Praise for the "Le

"[Jaime Lee Mann] captured a little bit of everything that's been really popular and intriguing for these readers."
- Karen Mair, CBC's *Mainstreet PEI* radio show

"This was an interesting fantasy read... It's fast paced, entertaining, and I found myself worrying about the two main characters."
- Jo Ann Hakola, aka The Book Faerie,
Journey of a Bookseller review blog

"I love the central plot in this book. It's a great world with some interesting characters and solid plot twists... a solid start to a series and likely to go over well with young fans of fantasy."
- Martha Dodge, *The One and Only Marfalfa* review blog

"This is a magical book of spells and goblins... From the opening page, the descriptions are so vivid!"
- Paul Alan, *House of Q* radio show

"Who knew you could throw so many curves into one hundred and fifty pages. This thrilling ride of sorcery and magic had the students in my class fully enveloped! I would recommend it to everyone, whether you are a grade four student or a grade four teacher!"
- Eric VanWiechen, grade four teacher,
Morell Consolidated School

"*Elora of Stone* is nothing like any other book I've ever read, I love it."
- Trysten, grade four student

"I really want to buy [*Elora of Stone*] whenever it comes out and never stop reading it."
- Jacob, grade four student

Copyright Information

Into Coraira (Legend of Rhyme Series Volume 1 Book 2)
Copyright 2015 by Jaime Lee Mann
ISBN 978-0-9947321-0-1 All rights reserved
Cover copyright: 2015 by Blue Moon Publishers
Cover design: Blue Moon Publishers
Editor: Christine Gordon Manley
Illustrations: Sarah Marie Lacy

Published in Canada by Blue Moon Voices, a division of Blue Moon Publishers, located in Toronto, Canada.

The author greatly appreciates you taking the time to read this work. Please consider leaving a review wherever you bought the book, or telling your friends or blog readers about the "Legend of Rhyme" series, to help spread the word. Thank you for your support.

Second Printing November 2015

INTO CORAIRA

By Jaime Lee Mann

BlueMoon
PUBLISHERS

TITLES IN THE "LEGEND OF RHYME" SERIES

For everyone who loved *Elora of Stone*

I wrote this book for you.

CONTENTS

INTRODUCTION

IF YOU read the first book in the "Legend of Rhyme" series, *Elora of Stone*, I'm sure you have lots of questions. Those questions will mostly be answered in the following chapters. (While you should still enjoy this book without having read *Elora of Stone*, I do highly recommend reading it in order to get the full Rhyme experience!)

In *Into Coraira*, you're going to find out what happened to all those missing infants, and you'll find out what happens with Asher's voice. But you'll also be taken on a whole new adventure as Ariana, Asher, and the entire realm of magic are faced with a new threat.

My daughters, Casey and Shelby, tell me they like this book even better than *Elora of Stone*. I wonder if you will agree.

Enjoy. And thank you for reading.

MAP OF RHYME

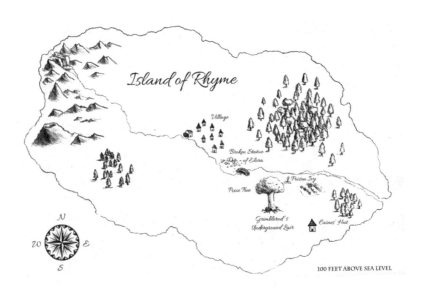

Island of Rhyme

Village

Broken Statue
of Elira

Pixie Tree

Poison Ivy

Grimblebrod's
Underground Lair

Caines' Hut

N
W E
S

100 FEET ABOVE SEA LEVEL

Once upon an enchanted land...

CHAPTER ONE - MIST

HIS BREATH hangs in clouds in the early morning air, the only sign that someone—or something—lurks among the rubble of Elora's fallen statue.

It's colder here than he remembers.

Once a powerful sorcerer, Asgall is weak in this form. For now, he is no more than vapour. If he doesn't feed on something soon to gain strength, he will die. And because mists do not have mouths, he can't feed until he finds a suitable host.

The realization hits him then. *I am free! Finally, I can have my revenge. And then I will pick up where I left off.*

Something whizzes past.

A flash of light drops to the ground where Asgall's feet should be.

The sinister mist watches two small creatures, neither bigger than a bird, explore the pile of grey rock. They have butterfly-like wings, iridescent like those of dragonflies. The female's wings twinkle blue, and her matching hair is tied back out of her face. The male isn't nearly as brightly coloured. His wings also twinkle, but his hair is a dull brown, and he has no unusual features to speak of, except for a spattering of freckles across the bridge of his nose.

Both beings are unaware of the living, breathing mist watching them.

What are these things?

"Thank goodness the rain has eased up," says the female. She effortlessly flips over a piece of rock the size of a loaf of bread. The rock lands in a puddle, splashing her friend with dirty water.

"Watch out, Sibley!" The male dries his face.

The mist sinks low, creeping along the rubble and around the creatures' feet. "This would be much easier in a couple of hours," grunts the male as he pushes a fragment of stone out of his way. "It's still dark!"

"Don't you think the humans might wonder how all the rocks are moving around on their own?" the female quips. She flies to her left, then to her right. "It should be here somewhere—"

"I think I see it!" The male flies just past the pile of stones.

The creature named Sibley joins him, where he stands over a shiny object almost his size.

"Yes, Cinnamon!" she says, leaning down and running her hands over the smooth surface of the stone. "It's definitely Elora's pendant."

Elora. They know Elora.

The mist drifts closer to the creatures, enveloping them. *One of these beings would make a suitable host. They're rather small, but they appear to be strong.*

"We better get this back to Calla," the thing called Cinnamon exclaims, wrapping the long gold chain around his waist. He picks up one end of the pendant and gestures for the Sibley one to do the same.

Did he say "Calla"? She is still among the living? Asgall pauses, straining to hear more.

"I've got it!" says the female, gripping her end of the pendant with both hands.

"Hurry, it's starting to rain again!" shouts the male.

Asgall swirls around the winged things.

The female freezes for a moment in mid-air and lifts her face to the sky, wrinkling her nose. "Do you smell that?"

Adscio! No, that isn't it. Asgall searches his memory for the spell.

The male looks up, and light raindrops splash on his face. "It almost smells like—"

Aciscio! breathes the mist. But nothing happens.

"It smells like evil magic. It must be from the remnants of the statue," the female shouts over the sound of the rain.

"Let's just get this pendant to Calla!" the male cries.

Before Asgall recalls the spell, the creatures race out of reach and are gone.

Thunderation! curses Asgall.

The pale morning sun peeks over the horizon into a dark grey sky. He grows increasingly angry. If mists had hearts, his would be pounding in his ears.

He drifts through the rocks below, scouring the ground for a host. In the wet grass just beyond the pile of rock, a robin plucks a reluctant worm from the earth.

That will do, thinks Asgall, watching the worm disappear down the robin's throat. *That will do fine.*

Asgall drifts closer to the bird.

This time, the words spill out of his invisible mouth. *Rapio! Insido! Occupo!*

And with that, Asgall is mist no more.

As his wings carry him into the pre-dawn sky, he promises himself that his enemies will regret the day they banished him into darkness.

CHAPTER TWO · WARNING

A UNICORN gallops through the open Coraira meadow, carrying the land's ruler, Calla, to the stream to meet Bardrick.

The long grass swishes and sways in the wake of the swiftly moving animal. Calla holds tightly to the unicorn's mane as they race to their destination. "We must hurry, Glint!" she says. "Faster!" They appear as a streak of white in a river of green with the unicorn's colouring, and Calla's flowing white gown and long golden hair.

A thought suddenly occurs to Calla. *Larque! He, too, needs to know of Asgall's escape.*

LARQUE PACES impatiently next to the pixie tree, waiting for Lochlan and Gwendolyn Caine to arrive as they'd arranged the night before. The tree is filled with bird and squirrel chatter. Their happy sounds contrast the sadness he feels over what he's been forced to do to protect the world from Elora.

"Larque." He hears Calla's voice in his ear. He closes his eyes to focus on her words.

I hear you, Calla.

"Have the pendants been given to Novah for the twins?"

Yes. His thoughts answer her question. *I am waiting now to meet with Lochlan and Gwendolyn.*

"Good. Now, though we should be celebrating last night's happy victory, I'm afraid we have a rather serious problem on our hands."

What is it?

"When the Darali portal opened for Elora, Asgall escaped," Calla explains.

I will come right away.

"No, first you must speak with the twins' parents as planned. And you must tell them the truth behind the legend. The whole truth. With the twins receiving their stones, they might prove invaluable if Asgall gets into Coraira. And we may need the support of their parents."

Are you sure?

"Yes. Come and join us after you speak with them. I am meeting Bardrick now to form a plan. I will see you soon."

HAVING PASSED the edge of the meadow, Glint canters through the forest, Calla's fingers twisting through the unicorn's mane.

"Mother, how I wish you were here to help at times like these," Calla whispers. But there is no answer. There hasn't been for hundreds of years, since she and her sister were little girls and their mother disappeared without a trace.

CHAPTER THREE - THE MORNING AFTER THE NIGHT BEFORE

"I CAN'T believe he is still sleeping!" Ariana Caine watches her twin brother snoozing on the straw mat in the corner of the hut.

"He needs his rest," Lochlan tells his daughter before a yawn escapes his own mouth. "We should all still be asleep after the night we put in."

"How did you find him, Ariana?" Gwendolyn whispers to her daughter.

Unlike her sleepy husband, Gwendolyn is bright and rested. There's a new softness in her smile. Her fair skin is almost glowing, and there's a twinkle in her blue eyes.

Ariana spreads a thick layer of raspberry jam on the warm slice of bread that sits on a plate in front of her and pours herself a cup of milk as she continues. "Yesterday, Sibley spoke to me while I was sitting on the shore, and I could see her as plain as day. She told me Asher was still alive, and I had to find him so we could help free Elora."

"Sibley knew about Asher?" gasps Gwendolyn. "Why hadn't she come to me before?"

"Sibley said she'd tried to talk to you many times about the possibility of Asher being alive, but you were unable to see her. She'd tried to get my attention, too, but for some reason she couldn't until yesterday," Ariana explains.

"Besides, nobody knew until last night where Asher was. Elora told us where to find him."

Lochlan frowns. "Why didn't you come to us so we could help find him?"

"Because we were running out of time," Ariana sighs. "We only had until midnight to find him and free Elora. But Elora lied, saying Larque was growing more powerful and had to be stopped. She said Asher was being kept underground, just past the pixie tree." Ariana takes a bite of bread and licks some sticky red jam from her finger.

"The pixie tree?" Lochlan asks.

"The big tree by the stream,"Ariana clarifies. "The one I used to love so much when I was a little girl."

"He was that close, all this time?" Gwendolyn puts her hands to her face.

Ariana nods.

The sound of straw rustling in the corner takes Gwendolyn and Lochlan's attention away from Ariana. Everyone falls silent as Asher begins to stir.

The boy slowly opens his eyes, squinting as they adjust to the light.

"Good morning, Asher," Gwendolyn quietly greets her son.

Is this what people do? Asher wonders as he rises to his feet. *Do they watch each other sleep?*

Ariana smiles at her brother's thought. "No," she says. "We've just been anxious to see you!"

Looking at her confused parents, Ariana reminds them about Asher's inability to speak and how they discovered the night before that they could read each other's minds.

A loud rumble comes from Asher's stomach.

"I don't need to read minds to know my boy is hungry!" Lochlan jumps to his feet. "I'll fix you some breakfast, son."

Lochlan snaps his fingers in the direction of the extinguished fire in the hearth. "Ignus!"

An orange flame dances up from the ashes.

Lochlan points at the bowl of brown and white eggs sitting on the table. "Attollo!"

Two eggs rise up out of the bowl.

As he moves his fingers in the direction of the pan, the eggs follow.

"Adflicto Affligo," he commands. The eggs crack themselves over the hot pan, landing with a sizzle. The shells set themselves neatly on the table.

Lochlan places two eggs on a plate for Asher, along with a leftover sausage and a large slab of honey cake. As he sets the plate on the table, there is a knock at the door.

"Ariana," says Gwendolyn as she pours a glass of milk for Asher, "would you mind seeing who it is?"

Ariana wipes her mouth and opens the door.

"Novah!" she cries, throwing her arms around the woman's neck.

"It's nice to see you, too, dear!" The woman standing at the door is shorter than Ariana. Her coarse grey hair is pinned up in a loose bun, and there is a smile in her kind brown eyes. A large cloth bag hangs from her shoulder. "Careful you don't squish the pie!"

"Yum! I'll take that!" Ariana takes the pie from Novah and holds it up to her nose, inhaling its sweet aroma.

"Novah!" Gwendolyn sets down the pitcher of milk. "What a wonderful surprise!"

"Hello, dear. Hello, all of you!" Novah's laughter fills the room.

Asher is crouched over his plate of eggs and sausage, scooping food into his mouth with his bare hands.

"I was so happy when I got your message!" Novah pulls a small scroll of parchment from her pocket and glances at Asher.

Noticing her husband's perplexed expression, Gwendolyn explains, "Last night, before sleep found me, I sent news about Asher to Novah and my parents. Lochlan, did you send word to Rebecca and Edmund?"

"I thought you would do that for me?" Lochlan teases.

Gwendolyn raises a dark brown eyebrow at her smirking husband.

"Yes," Lochlan says. "I used magic to send word to Mother last night. She hopes to visit soon, but Father is unable to come."

"Heavens," whispers Novah, "it looks like the poor child didn't eat the whole time he was down there!"

"I'm sure your pie will help fatten him up." Gwendolyn squeezes Novah's hand.

"Asher," Gwendolyn says, interrupting her son's meal, "do you remember Novah? She came to visit often when you were a little boy."

Asher looks up from his plate and wipes his mouth with his sleeve. He studies Novah's face for a moment before shaking his head.

"You would have been very young the last time you saw her, but Novah has been in our lives ever since your father and I moved to Rhyme," Gwendolyn explains.

"Children, can you guess why I've come today? Besides to lay my eyes again on young Asher, here!" Novah asks.

The twins shake their heads and look to their parents for a clue. But Lochlan and Gwendolyn shrug, unaware of Novah's agenda.

"I've come to give you your first magic lesson! How does that sound?"

"How did you know of their powers?" Lochlan asks.

Novah winks as she replies, "I am supplied with information as needed."

Ariana claps her hands. "Can we start right now?"

Asher smiles and nods eagerly.

"Gwendolyn, Lochlan," says Novah. "I know you're anxious to be reacquainted with your son, but I just left Larque by the pixie tree. He is ready to show you Coraira."

"Show us what?" Lochlan asks.

"The children, dear. He promised to explain what happened to the missing children. And they are in the magic realm. They are in Coraira."

CHAPTER FOUR - ORDERS

"DO YOU think Sibley and Cinnamon are ok?" Fidget wonders aloud from her perch within the branches of the pixie tree.

Wink scratches the back of his neck as he ponders his friend's question. "I'm sure we would have heard by now if they weren't."

"I feel a little rotten for leaving them there to fend for themselves last night, don't you?" Fidget glances sheepishly at Wink, nervously twisting one of her white braids between her tiny fingers.

Wink shrugs off the question. "Technically, it was you who left them there. I was just chasing after you to make sure you were all right. I was being a good friend. You were being a stinker."

Fidget frowns. "What do you think happened after we left?"

"You mean when Elora filled up the sky like giant, evil smoke? Hard to say." Wink sits back and crosses his arms in a contemplative pose. He pauses for a moment before speaking again. "Everyone's probably dead."

Fidget's green eyes grow wide. She brings the end of one of her braids to her mouth and bites down on it as Wink points to the sky.

"Oh look!" he says. "Sibley and Cinnamon are coming! They must not be dead after all."

The fairies land next to the pixies, balancing the pendant between them.

"Glad to see you two made it back ok," Cinnamon says. "You took off pretty quickly last night." He raises an eyebrow at the pixies.

"We were just talking about what might have happened after we left," says Fidget anxiously.

The fairies remain silent.

"So, what happened after we left?" asks Wink. "And what's that ya got there?" He points to the object the fairies are holding.

"Oh, this?" Sibley says, lifting her end of the pendant a little higher. "Just something Calla needs. And about last night," she continues, "we'll fill you in later. But it all turned out ok. Thank goodness."

"We better find Calla and get this to her," urges Cinnamon.

"Yes, but don't forget, we haven't yet given Fidget and Wink their assignment," whispers Sibley.

"What assignment?" Fidget and Wink ask in unison, no longer concerned about what happened after they abandoned the fairies.

"Well, to be perfectly honest," says Cinnamon to Sibley, "I don't think it's safe for them to go down there."

"Go down where?" Fidget pulls her red cap from the pocket of her flower petal skirt and sets it on her head.

"Did you see how they handled the ogre last night?" Sibley argues. "I think they can do it."

"What is it you want us to do?" Wink asks, nervously.

"Did you see how they ran away from Elora?" Cinnamon ignores Wink's question.

The pixies look at each other as the fairies debate. Wink makes some hand gestures and Fidget nods. The pixies then slowly slide their bodies along the branch of the tree, hoping the fairies won't notice their attempt to jump down and run away from any potentially dangerous task.

"Exactly! They recognized an opportunity to escape, and they took it," says Sibley. "That tells me they will flee Grimblerod's lair if they feel threatened."

Fidget loses her grip and slides down the tree branch in shock. "Grimblerod's lair?"

"Have you both gone completely mad?" Wink protests, jumping from the branch to the grass. "We can't go down there! He'll eat us alive! What are you thinking?"

"Oh Wink, you know goblins don't eat pixies," Sibley laughs, shifting her weight to keep the pendant balanced. "We haven't even told you what we need you to go down there for."

"Enlighten us," Wink replies. He crosses his arms defiantly over his chest and clenches his fists, growing increasingly flustered.

Cinnamon explains, "Calla and Sibley want you two to go into Grimblerod's lair to retrieve Asher's voice. I personally don't think you're cut out for such a challenge."

Fidget uses one of her braids to cover her eyes. "And you would be right!"

"Now hold on a red hot minute! What are you saying? What do you mean we're not cut out for such a challenge?" Wink shouts, insulted. "We are, and we accept it. Right, Fidget?"

Fear dances in Fidget's eyes as she looks hopelessly at Wink. "Really? This is going to happen?"

"You'll be fine!" says Sibley. "Think of the adventure it will be!"

Fidget's eyes narrow. "What do we have to do, exactly?" she asks.

"Well," explains Cinnamon, "Calla believes Grimblerod stole Asher's voice so the boy's cries wouldn't be heard above the ground. There's an old spell Grimblerod would have been capable of, which would have allowed him to store the voice in a crystal."

"Do we know this for sure?" asks Wink, suddenly taking his assignment quite seriously.

"Yes," Sibley says. "Calla has seen the spell before. She said the voice would probably be in the form of a sparkling blue crystal."

"I guess it shouldn't be too hard to find something sparkling down in those underground tunnels in the armpit of the earth," Wink says.

"Glad you're both on board. Now, we really must be going." Sibley nods at the pendant, then adds, "I would recommend you two wait on the human side of the tree until you see the old toad crawl out from his hole. The rain is easing up, and he'll want to be out where it's wet and mucky. Good luck."

Taking deep breaths, Fidget and Wink race to the trunk of the tree, which absorbs them one by one.

"I hope they'll be ok," sighs Cinnamon.

"You and me both," Sibley agrees. "Now let's get this pendant to Calla."

CHAPTER FIVE - THE PENDANT

THE PEGASUS' impressive wingspan momentarily blocks out the sun, casting a large shadow across the sparkling stream that runs through Coraira.

Calla emerges from the forest after having travelled across the magic realm in anticipation of Bardrick's arrival. She climbs down off Glint's back and lovingly rubs the animal's muzzle. The gleaming unicorn stands at its master's side, next to the water.

Golden hair cascades down Calla's back in soft waves. Her skin is creamy white and her eyes are as green as emeralds. She wears a crown of wild flowers, and a gauzy white dress flows around her bare feet.

She looks up at the bright blue sky with its soft purple and white clouds, watching the large winged horse make its graceful descent.

"Thanks for the ride, Panzer," Bardrick says, stroking the black mane of the white pegasus.

Panzer tucks his black and grey wings close to his body, allowing Bardrick to climb down from his back. He then gallops downstream to join a blessing of unicorns that splash in the sparkling water. Calla's unicorn remains by her side.

"Calla, it has been a long time," Bardrick says as he takes the woman's hand in his and kisses it.

Bardrick wears a neatly trimmed beard of brown whiskers, speckled with white and grey. His hair is short and slightly curly. His eyes are a deep brown, and his skin is tanned. His lips are drawn into a smile, revealing rows of gleaming white teeth.

"I wish it were more positive circumstances bringing us together," Bardrick says.

"As do I," Calla concurs.

"I suppose it's safe to assume he will be doing what he can to get his grimoire," says Bardrick.

Calla nods. "Yes. Of course, it has been well hidden. I don't suspect he will ever find it. But I am rather concerned about whether he will remain as a Darali mist, or if he will take the form of something or someone."

"Does he have any allies left among the living?" Bardrick asks.

"Not that I am aware of."

"We must ensure he does not get into Coraira. He will destroy it if he knows it is the source of the world's remaining magic," Bardrick states.

"He can't get in without a pendant," Calla reminds him.

"He can't get in as a *human* without a pendant," Bardrick corrects her. "But what if he takes the form of an animal or a fairy?"

Calla furrows her brow. "True. We do not know how powerful he will be. Here come the fairies with Elora's pendant." She gestures to the pixie tree. "The stones are all accounted for now... except for Freya's."

Sibley and Cinnamon fly from the pixie tree to the stream where Calla, Bardrick, and Glint stand, both with a firm hold on the pendant. They hover for a moment before landing on the unicorn's back.

"Sibley, Cinnamon." Calla approaches the fairies and extends her hands, over which the two drape the chain of the pendant.

"Do you both remember Bardrick?" Calla asks.

Both fairies nod in Bardrick's direction.

"Thank you both for your bravery," Bardrick says. "That must have been terribly frightening for you last night."

Sibley smiles shyly.

"And thank you for bringing this," he continues as he reaches down and touches the stone of Elora's pendant.

"I'm sure you're both wondering why you hadn't been told the truth about Elora," says Calla.

Both fairies look up at her, and Sibley speaks. "Yes, I can't help but think we may have been able to prevent what happened, had we known."

"Bardrick, Larque, and I agreed that the truth about Elora should be kept among us. We felt we could maintain better control over the situation if the Ancients were the only ones who knew about her," explains Calla.

"Couldn't we have been better prepared, had we known?" Sibley asks.

"We needed you fairies to believe it was Elora's accidental curse that was sending the missing twins to Coraira," Calla adds. "We feared that if the fairies knew what Larque and Grimblerod were doing, the truth would spread to the human realm."

Calla pauses, then says, "Besides, we believed that by keeping twins apart, we wouldn't have to worry about Elora being released. The curse Larque put her under was secure. Everything happened very quickly last night, and when Larque tried to explain that Elora was not to be trusted, nobody would believe him."

"We truly thought Larque was the threat," Sibley says in a soft voice as she twirls the unicorn's fur between her fingers.

"I am sorry, Sibley," sighs Calla. "Perhaps we didn't make the right decision, and I do hope you will forgive me and the others. But for now, there's something both of you need to know."

Bardrick's jaw is set. His face takes on a hard appearance.

Calla's hands close tightly around Elora's pendant.

"As you've both likely guessed," Calla says, "Bardrick is here for a reason." She searches for the right words. "When Elora was sent to Darali, the portal was open long enough to let a great evil back through into the human realm. The sorcerer Asgall has escaped."

Bardrick now speaks. "We don't know what form he may take or where he might be, but his rage has been bottled up for centuries, and he will be thirsty for revenge against me for sending him into darkness."

"Who is Asgall?" Cinnamon asks.

Calla closes her eyes before speaking. "He is the most evil sorcerer who has ever lived. And he is also my father."

CHAPTER SIX - THE WOMAN

SHE TUCKS a long strand of hair behind her ear as she stirs the broth. Leaning over the cauldron, she inhales the rich aroma, steam covering her face.

The vision appears as she unties her apron. It comes in a flash at first. It takes her only a moment to recognize what's happening. She closes her eyes and lets the vision unfurl.

A common robin sits beneath an evergreen tree. Its yellow beak pierces a thick layer of pine needles.

Its voice now fills her head. *Can you hear me?*

"Yes," the woman answers. Her eyes are still closed. "Is that you, Asgall? It's been so long since you've made contact," she says with surprise.

There's no time for small talk, replies Asgall. *I have made it back to your realm. I'm trying to gain strength. Do you know the whereabouts of my grimoire?*

"No."

I left it hidden in my lair on the island of Rhyme. You must look for it there.

"Then, what?" the woman asks.

My grimoire has the power to bring to life anything within its pages. With it, I will once again be at the height of my power. Then, I can resume my work. I will need you to help me carry out the plan I was working on when Bardrick and Freya sent me to the darkness.

I would have preferred Elora's assistance, but I understand something has happened to her.

"Elora was banished to Darali last night. It was a pair of twins who freed her," she says, "and twins who sent her to the darkness."

I see. Perhaps, when my plan is complete, I can rescue her. But first ... I must seek a more suitable host while you find the grimoire. Tell me more about these twins?

"The power of Asher and Ariana Caine will be of epic proportions."

Seek them out, as you search for my grimoire. Learn more about them.

"Yes, Asgall," the woman replies. "And then?"

Patience. Have patience. Soon I'll be able to control all magic, and use it for our own gains.

"Asgall, since you've been gone, things have changed. In order to control magic, you need to gain entry to Coraira."

Coraira?

"It is the realm of magic. It was sealed off from the human realm to prevent you from entering. But you might be able to gain entry in your current form."

I see someone. Asgall has become distracted.

Larque.

The vision goes black, leaving the woman with nothing to watch but the backs of her eyelids.

She opens her eyes and removes the cauldron from its hook over the fire, placing it on the counter. It will be a day's journey to Rhyme, using traditional modes of travel. *I will need to use magic,* she tells herself.

She pulls her own grimoire from one of the shelves on the wall and flips to a page showing a map of Rhyme. She sets the book on the table and faces the bottles on the wall. She selects three and sets them next to the book.

This is my chance to be great, she thinks, a smile rising to her lips. *To have the power I always deserved.*

After slinging a cloth bag over her shoulder, she takes an empty glass bottle and drops in small amounts of liquids from the other three. A blue mist curls up out of the mouth of the bottle.

She holds the grimoire open to the map of Rhyme and drinks the simple potion. And, then, she is gone.

CHAPTER SEVEN - QUEST

"HOW DO we know we haven't missed him already?" Fidget wrinkles her face as she asks Wink the question he's also been asking himself.

She and Wink have been watching for Grimblerod for what feels like hours.

"I dunno. Should we just go down there already?" Wink suggests. At that very moment, a green-brown head squeezes through a hole at the base of the pixie tree.

As the large toad hops away from the tree, Fidget softly whispers, "Are we sure about this?"

"Nope. But we have no choice, so let's go!" Wink says, jumping to the ground.

Fidget hesitates before bouncing down from the branch and following Wink into the hole that leads to Grimblerod's lair.

"Ouch!" moans Wink as Fidget lands on top of him in the dark.

"Sorry!" Fidget squeals as she tries to find her footing.

The pixies dust themselves off and quickly survey their surroundings. Torches hang from the dirt walls of the tunnel, providing a dim source of light.

"I can't believe that boy really lived down here," Wink says with a shudder, studying the shadows he and Fidget cast on the tunnel wall. "It's so dark and creepy."

"And it smells like rotten old toad slime," whispers Fidget.

"Ok, let's try to focus," urges Wink. "We're looking for a blue crystal."

The pixies walk in silence for a moment. The only sounds they hear in the underground tunnel are their own breath and a steady drip of water coming from somewhere in the depths of the earth.

"Fidget! A door!" Wink whispers suddenly, stopping in his tracks.

"Aw, I adore you, too!" gushes Fidget.

"Not adore, you nincompoop. A d-o-o-r door!" Wink points to a brass doorknob attached to a large, rounded wooden door. Of course, the door seems large to them because of their small size. It would be quite short to a human.

"Oh look! A door!" cries Fidget. "It must lead to Grimblerod's cave!"

Fidget doesn't see Wink roll his eyes in the dark.

"Hop on my shoulders so you can reach the doorknob," says Wink.

With one bounce, Fidget hops easily onto her friend's shoulders, and, from there, she hops again to get a grip on the cool brass doorknob.

Fidget wraps her arms around the top of the knob, struggling to make it turn.

"A little help here?" she cries out to her friend.

"Hold on!" instructs Wink, taking a step back. With Fidget dangling from the doorknob, he gives her foot a good tug.

"AAAAAAHH! I'm getting awfully dizzy!" Fidget continues to hold on tightly to the knob. Wink pulls her foot again, and they finally hear a click. The door slowly creaks open.

Fidget jumps down to the ground. "Are we really going in there?" she asks.

But her question goes unanswered because Wink has already crept inside Grimblerod's cave.

Fidget sighs and tiptoes through the open door. "Wow! That old Grimblerod is quite a good housekeeper," she muses. "Everything is in order in here. Maybe he could help us clean our place, eh, Wink?"

She waits for a response before whispering slightly louder, "Hey, Wink, are you still here?"

"Over here!" a voice replies from deeper within the cave.

Looking up, Fidget sees a vast network of wispy, white tree roots reaching through the dirt and stretching across the ceiling.

Insects scurry around her feet as she tiptoes through the damp cave. "I'm not sure I care for it down here," Fidget whispers, spitting out a sticky wad of spider web that's drifted into her mouth.

"Hey, what's that?" asks Wink, pointing to a rough work bench that has been fashioned out of twigs. On top of the bench is a pile of small bones, a rusty nail, a gold coin, and a bright blue crystal.

Fidget gasps loudly and looks from her arm to the bones on the bench. "Those are the size of pixie bones!"

"No, no, no, Fidget. Remember, goblins don't eat pixies," Wink scolds. "At least I don't think they do. Anyway, I'm talking about that sparkly blue crystal!"

Wink jumps onto the bench and swipes up the crystal, which is about the size of an acorn. The small pixie holds it tightly in both hands and leaps back down, joining Fidget on the ground.

"Great! We have the crystal," claps Fidget. "Ooooooh, look!"

A thin wooden door on the opposite side of the cave catches Fidget's attention. It's quite short, even to a pixie.

"Whaddaya think's in here?" Fidget asks, running her hand along the smooth wood.

"Come on, Fidget, we have to go! We have the crystal!" Wink urges.

"I can't help it! I have to open it!" Fidget pulls on the doorknob.

"No, let's go!" cries Wink.

Despite her friend's objections, Fidget pulls on the doorknob as hard as she can. "It's double-darn-it stuck!"

As her words fill the air, the door finally gives, and an avalanche of crystals pours out, covering both pixies.

"Now, look what you've done! I've dropped it!" Wink screams. He looks around and sees hundreds of crystals in every colour of the rainbow. Except blue.

"What do you think you're doing?" a muffled voice spits at the pixies from behind.

Fidget and Wink struggle to their feet in the shimmering pile of crystals, but neither are brave enough to turn around and face the source of the voice.

"Wink, please tell me your voice has gotten deeper," Fidget squeaks.

"I'm afraid to look," whispers Wink, with his hands over his eyes.

Fidget spins around slowly and sees a long claw-like toenail. Her face is almost level with the goblin's knees, which are caked black with dirt. She is close enough to smell the cheesy stench coming from his feet. Taking a few steps back, Fidget looks up at the old goblin. Her knees are shaking.

"I don't care for pixies above the ground," sneers Grimblerod, "but I will not stand for them snooping around in my home."

"It's not like that! We fell down into one of your holes," Wink insists. "We were just trying to find our way out!"

"Then allow me to help you," Grimblerod says as he pushes Wink backwards with his long dirty fingernail.

"No need!" cries Wink. "We'll be fine!"

"What are all of these?" Fidget asks the goblin, motioning to the pile of crystals.

Wink glares at his friend. "Fidget, let's go!"

"The souls of all the pixies I've caught down here over the years," Grimblerod replies. "Now LEAVE! Unless you want to join the pile."

Grimblerod's toenails scratch in the dirt.

"Run!" shouts Wink.

Fidget and Wink race through Grimblerod's feet and down the tunnel.

"I see light!" Wink exclaims. Fidget feels wind as Grimblerod's hand swipes at them.

Fidget and Wink push through a curtain of black and blue insect wings that hangs to the floor. It makes a soft clicking sound as it sways out of their way.

"We're going the wrong way!" cries Fidget.

The pixies change direction and race again over the goblin's feet.

"A way out!" cries Wink, pointing at the ceiling.

"We can't jump that high!" replies Fidget in dismay, looking up at the hole about ten feet above them.

The pixies flinch, hearing Grimblerod's grunts as he pushes through the insect wing curtain into the cave where he had kept Asher Caine.

"Climb!" Wink takes a giant leap and clings to the dirt wall. Fidget does the same.

The pixies scale the wall, digging their tiny fingers into the soil while their feet slip on the mossy coating Grimblerod put there to prevent Asher from climbing out.

"Hey, Wink," pants Fidget, struggling to keep from sliding back down into the cave.

"Ya?" grunts Wink. He has almost reached the opening.

"Don't you wish pixie dust was a thing?"

"Let's ask Calla about that," suggests Wink as he climbs up out of the hole.

Firmly planted on the ground, Wink reaches into the hole, extending his hand to Fidget. Accepting her friend's offer of help, Fidget climbs up onto the grass.

Satisfied that the intruders have left without any valuables, Grimblerod shouts, "And stay out!" before disappearing back behind the insect wing curtain.

The pixies race back to the tree and shimmy up the trunk to their watching place—their entry point to Coraira.

After taking a minute to catch her breath, Fidget looks at Wink. "So, we messed that one up pretty good, didn't we?"

Wink looks down his nose at Fidget. "You shouldn't have opened that door!"

"What are we going to do now, without a crystal?"

"Fidget?" asks Wink, sticking out his belly, which appears to be three times its normal size. "Notice anything different about me?"

"Wink! Are you having a baby? I'm gonna be an auntie!" Fidget squeals with her hands up near her face. "Hey, wait. You're a boy. Boys can't have babies."

Exhausted, Wink reaches under his white wool shirt and pulls out a dazzling crystal.

"You got it!" Fidget cheers.

"No, Fidget," Wink says sadly, "I didn't."

Taking a closer look, Fidget sees that the crystal in Wink's hands is green.

CHAPTER EIGHT · GIFTS

NOVAH AND the twins stand at the door of the hut, watching Lochlan and Gwendolyn walk, hand-in-hand, to the pixie tree.

"I thought they'd never leave!" Novah laughs. She coaxes the twins to a soft patch of grass, not far from the berry bushes that surround the property.

The rain has completely stopped. The sun is shining and the air is warm. Only a few wisps of clouds float across the pale blue sky.

"Oh, the grass is wet," Novah says. "That won't do!" She lifts her arms out to her sides, clears her throat, and says, "Beads of water made from rain, rise up to the clouds again!"

Millions of raindrops float up off the ground in slow motion. The sun shines through them, filling each one with softly glowing yellow light.

The enchanted beads of water clink like soft chimes when they touch.

"There." Novah pushes the long skirt of her plain brown dress to one side and takes a seat on the dry grass. The beads of water continue to float up to the clouds.

Ariana and Asher remain standing, transfixed by the glowing drops of water that surround them. Novah motions for them to take a seat beside her.

"Novah, why have I never seen you do magic before?" Ariana asks.

"The time hadn't come until now, dear child."

"Why now?" Ariana asks what her brother is also thinking.

"What I did just now with the rain? That's an example of one of my gifts," Novah explains with a twinkle in her brown eyes. "I have a certain amount of... er... control over the elements. And you each have gifts and powers of your own. I can now show you my magic because now is the time for me to teach you yours."

Asher's face breaks into a wide grin. Ariana squeals and claps her hands together.

Novah reaches into her cloth bag and pulls out two small satin pouches. One is emerald green and the other is royal blue. Each has the letter "A" embroidered on it in gold thread and is tied shut with a length of gold cord with tasseled ends.

"These are for you." Novah hands the green bag to Asher and the blue one to Ariana.

The twins carefully untie their pouches and pull out nearly identical opal pendants.

"It's beautiful!" Ariana exclaims, examining hers. Tiny strands of colour—oranges, pinks, blues, and greens—all swirl around within the stone as if it was both liquid and solid at the same time.

Asher shakes his pendant and holds it to his ear. *What is this for?* he wonders.

With a hearty laugh, Novah corrects him. "It's to be worn like this!"

Novah drapes the pendant around Asher's neck. She places her hand on the stone. "They look the same, but they have slightly different properties."

"You mean they do something?" Ariana puts on her own pendant and admires the opal inside, running her fingers over its smooth surface.

"Why yes, dear," says Novah. "These pendants have come from the magic realm of Coraira. The ruler of Coraira herself asked Larque to give these to you. He then entrusted them to me to pass on."

"Why us? What do they do?" asks Ariana.

Novah beams at the twins. "These pendants are going to help me see what gifts you possess. You are so special, both of you. In fact, did you know that your arrival was the most magically significant birth in centuries?"

Ariana and Asher exchange looks. "What does that mean? 'Magically significant'?" Ariana speaks for both of them.

"What that means, children, is that your powers are on the same level as those of the Ancients. Formidable magicians like Larque and Elora. Though, surely, your magic will be on the side of light and not dark."

"How do you know this?" Ariana asks, tilting her head. Beside her, Asher squints in confusion.

"Calla, the ruler of the magic realm, told me," Novah says, shifting her weight to get comfortable on the grass.

Does this mean we're going to be evil, like Elora? Asher's thoughts turn to fear.

"Asher, dear, I don't believe either of you will become evil. Your mother is a pure heart, for starters, but the decision will ultimately be yours whether you choose to practice good magic or dark magic. You would have to make the choice to be evil. I don't believe that's a choice either of you will make."

"Why don't you or Father have pendants?" Ariana asks.

"It simply wasn't to be for us," Novah says with a smile.

"Can we learn our powers now?" pleads Ariana.

"Give me your hands, dear," says Novah. Ariana does as instructed.

Novah looks into Ariana's eyes, then back to her palms. After a moment, Novah speaks. "Oh my."

"What is it?" Ariana inquires excitedly.

"You, my child, with your pure heart and ability to feel things so deeply—you have a very powerful gift indeed. And you must always and forever be mindful of what you say. For you, my dear Ariana, you have the power to make wishes come true."

Looking at her own hands, Ariana is stunned. "I can make wishes come true? Real, actual wishes?"

"Yes, dear," Novah confirms. "I must admit I'm rather shocked myself! This is a very powerful gift, and you will need to learn to control it."

Could Ariana have wished me back home? Asher thinks.

"Brother, I wished for your return many times," Ariana says with a frown.

"Oh, Asher." Novah drapes her arms around his shoulders. "Your sister had no idea she had this type of power, and she still has to be taught how to use it! Even if she had known she possessed this gift, she wouldn't have known how to employ it."

Looking back to Ariana, Novah continues, "Child, you must always be aware of this gift. Wishing certain things to happen could break the rules of magic."

"What rules?"

"Most types of magic come with a cost. Rules must be followed in order for a certain level of balance to be maintained. For instance, the way I made the grass dry earlier? That was not affecting the bigger picture. But had I made it rain? Well, rain is dictated by nature. That would be something that would need to be counter-balanced. If someone forced a rain, perhaps a drought would occur elsewhere, or maybe the temperature would rise to unnatural levels."

"How do you know all of these things, Novah?" asks Ariana, looking into Novah's kind, familiar face. "Are you a witch?"

"Yes, I am, dear. Though I never cared for that word. I am a trusted friend of the Ancients. I knew there was something special about you, Ariana, since you were a small child. It was no surprise when Larque told me about the magic between you and Asher. The energy that comes from you two is quite remarkable."

Novah turns to Asher. "Now, Asher, would you like to know what your gift is?"

Nodding, Asher gives Novah his hands.

Asher's pendant glows as Novah looks from his palms into his eyes.

"Asher. You have also been given a powerful gift, dear boy."

His green eyes look expectantly at Novah.

"You have a gift that I haven't seen in anyone but Larque. You, Asher, have the ability to manipulate time."

What does that mean? Asher wonders.

"I think it means that you can make time move!" Ariana says, with a hint of amazement in her voice. "But is that really possible?"

"Yes, Asher, Ariana is right. You will be able to move time backwards and forwards, at least to an extent. Larque's ability is limited to pausing time."

Novah gazes at the twins intently. "Both of you have gifts that are extremely powerful. You will be at risk of breaking the laws of magic," Novah cautions. "We must start your lessons right away."

CHAPTER NINE - ANOTHER WORLD

"I'D HOPED we would have more time together this morning, but I'm afraid a rather pressing matter has come up, and I'm needed elsewhere very shortly," Larque tells Lochlan and Gwendolyn when they arrive at the pixie tree. "However, I told you I would explain what happened to all of those twins, and I will do as I promised."

"Is everything all right?" Gwendolyn asks.

"I hope it will be. But we've suddenly been faced with a great threat. The sorcerer Asgall has escaped his imprisonment."

"Who is Asgall?" Lochlan asks.

"A very dangerous being," says Larque. "Asgall is Elora and Calla's father. During his time, he was solely responsible for causing a famine, just to see how many he could kill without using his actual hands. And that's just a small example of his evil nature. He once tried to raise the sea level to completely obliterate the human race. Luckily, Freya managed to stop him in time."

"And he is here now?" Lochlan gasps.

"The children—" Gwendolyn starts, her eyes wide.

"The children are safe with Novah. Her powers are strong enough to keep them protected," Larque says. "Besides, Asgall has been in Darali a long time, and he will need to gain strength. Now, as I'm sure you both understand, this matter is weighing heavily on my mind. I would like to explain to you now what happened to the twins, so that I can be where I'm needed."

"Of course," Gwendolyn nods. "But this can wait! Isn't it more important that you be searching for Asgall?"

"It all ties together, Gwendolyn. I've been instructed to tell you both more about the legend of Rhyme in case we need your help later," Larque says.

"Then let us waste no more time," Lochlan states, inviting Larque to continue.

"Grimblerod takes the form of a toad when he goes above ground," Larque begins. "Except during the full moon, when he is able to surface as a goblin. Grimblerod had to be in goblin form in order to replace a twin with one of his enchanted wooden dolls."

"So, this is why babies were always lost at different ages?" Gwendolyn asks.

"Yes," replies Larque, "though we tried to ensure babies were taken as close to birth as possible. Not only because it made it easier for Grimblerod to handle the infants, as he's not very large, but also so the remaining twin wouldn't experience such a sense of loss."

"Please, what happened to these babies?" Gwendolyn urges with tears in her eyes.

"In the morning," Larque continues, "the parents would wake to a lifeless child. Grimblerod, however, brought the babies back here to this tree and placed them in an enchanted glass box, built centuries ago by an elder dwarf. The box served as a vessel and transported the babies to Calla."

"Right," Lochlan says, "Elora's twin who we all believed to be dead."

"Yes," Larque confirms. "As I explained last night, the legend of Rhyme is not based entirely on fact. Elora, Calla, and myself belong to a small group of witches and wizards known as the Ancients. Asgall was one of the oldest of our kind. We have long kept the truth among us to protect magic, leaving humans to believe the legend. It was thought to be the only way to keep all of the realms secure."

"What do you mean, all of the realms?" Gwendolyn asks.

"Humans are only aware of this earthly realm, but there are others. There's also the dark realm of Darali, the magic realm of Coraira, and of course, the spirit realm or the final resting place. Elora was sent to Darali last night. Calla is in Coraira."

"How did all of these realms come to be?" asks Lochlan.

"Darali and Coraira were created by Bardrick, an Ancient as old as Asgall. It was Bardrick, along with Asgall's own wife, Freya, who sent Asgall to Darali. Soon after Asgall was banished, Bardrick went to work on his plan to seal off magic from the rest of the world." Larque pauses and touches his pendant.

"And where is Freya now?" Gwendolyn asks.

"She is in hiding," Larque says. "When Asgall was sent to Darali, Freya was terrified he would come back for her and their daughters. She left Elora and Calla to be raised by a human couple, and then she simply vanished."

"So, Freya was good?" Lochlan clarifies.

"Yes, and when Freya and Asgall first met, Asgall was not yet practicing dark magic. He grew evil over the years. The stronger he got, the darker he became."

"How did Calla end up in Coraira?" Gwendolyn asks.

"When she was barely a teenager, Calla was chosen by Bardrick to rule the magic realm he'd created, so he could be left to guard the portals between the realms. Everyone was led to believe that Calla had died, to explain her disappearance, and to further protect Coraira."

"So, the children are in this protected magic realm," Gwendolyn says. "Doesn't this mean we can reunite them with their parents?"

"I'm afraid it isn't quite that easy," Larque says.

"Why not? If the children are fine?" Gwendolyn asks.

"Even if this feat were possible, remember, Gwendolyn, that many of the twins were separated hundreds of years ago. The parents are not necessarily still here waiting for their children to return."

Gwendolyn frowns as Larque continues. "Calla and I are able to communicate through our thoughts, across time and distance. Shortly after Elora banished me, Calla and I collaborated on a plan we believed to be best for the children and the family members left behind. All while keeping the world safe from Elora—neither of us wanted her to be released from stone."

"What did you do?" Lochlan asks, squeezing Gwendolyn's hand.

Larque takes a deep breath before he continues his explanation. "We wanted the twins to know they had parents who loved them—for them to know where they came from. Calla was admiring a glass wing butterfly while she was holding the first of these babies. Glass wing butterflies are an enchanted species. They carry magic from Coraira to wherever it's needed." He pauses to allow Gwendolyn and Lochlan a moment to absorb this information.

"It was Calla who had the idea to give these children some of the magical properties of the glass wing butterflies."

"Wait. Are we to understand that you turned the children into butterflies?" Lochlan asks.

"No. Not exactly," says Larque. "When Calla held one of these babies, she would choose the perfect butterfly match for him or her. She would place the butterfly on the child's chest, right above his or her heart. Then, she would recite the spell we wrote together. A tiny enchanted creature was born as a result—a blend of human and butterfly. A miniature human with wings. The colouring of the butterfly would determine the features of this new being."

"You created fairies," Gwendolyn whispers.

"Yes," confirms Larque. "Fairies reach maturity in only a couple of human days and they are ageless. Calla raised the fairies to be kind and good. They have the enchantment of glass wing butterflies, so they can travel freely between realms. They spread magic like the butterflies do. Calla put an enchantment on the fairies so they could not be seen by humans. For humans don't always respect magic."

"So, the twins became fairies," Gwendolyn says again.

"Yes, each fairy became a guardian for his or her human twin," Larque explains. "And because they were able to fly freely through the human world, Calla tasked them with the responsibility of keeping an eye on all children. If you ever narrowly escaped a great accident or some sort of grave danger, that was quite likely a watcher fairy intercepting the threat."

"All my life," Gwendolyn muses, "when I avoided an accident, I would see a flash of blue light. I never got hurt, even as a child. Was that Sibley?"

Larque nods. "Or another fairy. But it's because of your pure heart that you were ever able to see fairies at all. Most humans, even children, can't see them."

"Why do Ariana and Asher have fairy guardians?" Lochlan asks.

"Your own fairy guardians became theirs. Calla knew that Ariana and Asher must be guarded very closely because of their powerful magic."

"So, Asher's watcher..." Lochlan pauses.

"Cinnamon," Larque finishes.

"Yes, Cinnamon," Lochlan says. "He is my brother?"

"He is," Larque answers.

"I wish I could see him," says Lochlan.

Gwendolyn squeezes his hand.

"Now that you know what happened to those babies, would you like to see where they live?" Without waiting for an answer, Larque raises his arms and starts to speak before something catches his attention from the corner of his eye.

Lochlan and Gwendolyn turn to see what he is looking at, but all they see is a robin bobbing around the base of the tree.

"What is it, Larque?" Lochlan asks.

"I'm not sure," Larque states. "It's probably nothing."

Larque looks long and hard at the robin before raising his arms again to reveal Coraira.

He faces the tree and stares at it intently. "Coraira," he orders, "reveal yourself."

The air in front of Lochlan and Gwendolyn shimmers and ripples like water.

The tree disappears from sight, as does everything else around them.

"Welcome to Coraira."

When the ripples stop, Lochlan and Gwendolyn are standing in what seems to be the same place in which they were a moment ago, but now they are immersed in paradise. There is a forest east of the pixie tree, with tangles of trees forming an archway leading into what can only be described as an enchanted wood.

Lochlan and Gwendolyn see a stream that appears to be the same one that runs through Rhyme. They also spy the same rocky mountainous range far off in the distance to the west.

A rainbow stretches across the sky, half of it buried behind the mountain, the other end dipping down into the stream where the water sparkles in the sun. A group of winged horses and unicorns drink from the twinkling water.

Birds of all different colours perch in tree branches. Flowers sprout up all around, their faces of blue, purple, and white attracting dozens of different types of butterflies and bumblebees.

"Larque," Gwendolyn whispers after a moment. "This is like something from a dream! This is where the fairies live?"

"It is," nods Larque.

"Who are those people?" Lochlan asks, pointing to a man and woman standing near the sparkling stream.

"That would be Calla and Bardrick. As I said, they are waiting for me."

Calla and Bardrick, sensing Larque's presence, look over in his direction.

The pendant that hangs around Larque's neck glows and starts to rise from his chest as if by some magnetic force.

Larque touches the stone. "I really must go. I've kept them waiting long enough."

"Wait, Larque, before you go... what will happen if Asgall gets into Coraira?" Lochlan asks.

"I suspect he will destroy Calla. And without a successor, without Calla, magic will cease to exist."

"When you find Asgall, will you kill him?" asks Lochlan.

"If only it were that easy," Larque says.

Leaving the Caines with their heads full of questions, Larque states, "Regelo!" and walks into the scene of Coraira.

Around Lochlan and Gwendolyn, the air ripples again. Coraira disappears.

Rhyme appears as it did before.

Except that the robin is no longer there.

CHAPTER TEN - THE RIVALRY

CORAIRA IS even more overwhelming to Asgall's long-dormant senses than the human realm was.

He hops through the grass, for he has not yet grown fond of flying.

He feels warmth as his feathers soak up heat from the bright Coraira sun. There was no sun in Darali. There was nothing there but endless black.

He flaps his wings and flies towards Larque, remaining as close as he can to the ground.

He smiles to himself. *I learned more than I thought I would as this ridiculous bird. What good timing it was that I was so close to the portal when I spotted Larque.*

He sees her then. Standing beside a unicorn.

Pale blond hair shining in the sun. A crown of flowers on her head. Her long white dress flows out around her feet, making it look as though she could float across the ground. She's more beautiful than he remembers.

So good. So kind.

Such a disappointment.

The robin hops closer.

Bardrick.

Asgall is enveloped in rage. He hops closer to his enemy.

His memory takes him back to that day, so many years ago that he couldn't begin to count them.

He can still hear the ungodly scream that rose up out of the volcano's throat before he willed it to erupt, like a kettle whistle so loud it could deafen you. He can smell the sulphuric, ashy stench of it. Can remember how the cloud of smoke that rose up and out of the cone filled the sky.

The scorching hot lava poured down the volcano's flank, promising to destroy everything in its path.

Asgall remembers how powerful he felt in that moment. He'd simply sketched an erupting volcano in his grimoire and recited the spell. He had reached the point where he could control nature.

As the volcano continued to spew molten rock, it made a sound like a rapid, muffled heartbeat. Like the sound of a baby's heart beating in its mother's belly.

He couldn't wait to show Freya what he'd done. How powerful her husband had become. When he beckoned her to his mountainside lair, he'd expected her to be happier than she'd been. He remembers how beautiful she was. Hair black as night poured like silk down her back. Her olive skin was smooth and youthful. But her ice-blue eyes were full of fear. Ash rained down from the sky. It didn't land on her, but it fell all around her.

"Asgall," she said in a quiet voice, "what have you done?"

His grimoire was sitting on the ground beside him. Its pages were opened to the sketch of the volcano. Freya picked up the book.

It was at that moment that Bardrick appeared. His oldest friend. *Ha. Some friend he'd turned out to be.*

"I'm sorry it happened this way," Freya said. "I did love you once."

"What is happening?" Asgall recalls the feeling of complete hopelessness he had experienced as he watched Freya vanish into thin air with his grimoire.

"No! What do you think you're doing?" he hissed.

"Asgall," Bardrick said, "you have taken this too far."

Asgall extended his arms in Bardrick's direction, and that's the last thing he remembers before being hurled into endless darkness. Whatever spell Bardrick had developed had been powerful, and it caught him off guard.

He would not be taken by surprise again.

CHAPTER ELEVEN - THE PLAN

LARQUE FACES Calla and Bardrick. "Where do we even start to look for him?"

Calla twists her hands together. "We expect he will seek out his grimoire."

"There's really no telling the type of evil he may unleash with that book, having been locked away in the dark for so long," adds Larque.

"But he will never find it," states Bardrick. "The grimoire is with the other relics in the sea dragon's cave."

Sibley and Cinnamon appear suddenly and hover before Calla. "Shall we warn the other creatures of Asgall's escape?" Cinnamon asks.

"Yes, thank you," Calla says.

A curious robin hops closer to the Ancients as the fairies fly off.

"Wait, do you both smell that?" Bardrick sniffs.

Calla and Larque exchange worried glances. "Yes," Larque says. "Sulphur."

Calla's green eyes laser in on the robin looking up at them.

A jolt of fear rises within Asgall, and he flies off, knowing he's been spotted. He feels a buzz of electricity whip past him, close enough to move his feathers.

Asgall swoops to the ground so he can stop and observe what's happening. With his clawed yellow feet gripped safely to the earth, he peers up from the blades of grass to see Calla with her arms extended in his direction. Light emanates from her fingertips. It is aimed at him.

That miserable child. Asgall bounces out of the way of the beams of white being shot in his direction.

Trying to destroy her own father. Perhaps she's more like me than I thought.

Ouch!

One of his beady black eyeballs sees that smoke is rising from his tail feathers.

The eye on the other side of his head notices a slender yellow snake slithering through the grass.

Much better. Asgall smiles.

A sinister mist rises from the robin and swirls for a moment in the air before entering the mouth of the snake.

"FRIGIDUS IN tempore!" Larque shakes his hands in the direction of the robin. The bird freezes in mid-flap.

Bardrick, Calla, and Larque walk briskly to the place where the robin is suspended.

Bardrick reaches up and plucks it from the air. He sticks his hand into one of his pockets and pulls out a drawstring bag. He starts to place the bird inside.

"Wait," prompts Calla. "The smell is fading."

They all look now at the robin.

"If this was Asgall, we would smell the darkness. He has escaped again," Bardrick concludes. "And he heard us divulge the location of the grimoire."

Bardrick shakes his fingers over the robin, and the bird ruffles its feathers before flying off, confused.

Bardrick hands Elora's pendant to Larque. "Starla will be waiting for you at the dragon cave. She has a vessel to hide the pendant in. While you're there, you must retrieve the grimoire."

Bardrick whistles for Panzer. "I'm glad you're back, Larque," he states. "Calla can use your help. I must get back to the portal so nothing else can escape." He lifts himself onto the back of the pegasus and they fly up towards the portal to Darali. In a matter of seconds, they can no longer be seen.

"Larque, while you hide the pendant and retrieve the grimoire, I'll start working on a locator spell. He could be anywhere... or anything. And I also must prepare for what will happen in the event that Asgall is not captured in time."

"I will be back soon." Larque plants a kiss on Calla's hand.

Calla then watches as Larque disappears from sight, transporting himself to the western side of the island, to the sea dragon's cave, in a blink of light.

CHAPTER TWELVE - REVENGE SOUGHT

GRIMBLEROD GRUNTS as he picks up the crystals that were disturbed moments ago by the blasted pixies. The brightly coloured gems clink together, filling the empty tunnels with a musical echo.

The goblin brings the back of his hand to his face and wipes dusty grime from his eyes. As he shuffles through the lair, he feels a buzzing from within his pocket. The green stone is vibrating. He pulls the stone from his pocket and puts it to his forehead.

When he closes his eyes, a vision of Larque appears. *Grimblerod.*

"Yes," the goblin mumbles.

Asgall has escaped.

A prickly heat rises up from Grimblerod's belly to his face. He hasn't heard that name in a hundred years or more, but he has thought of him every day. Asgall. The monster. The man who ruined his life.

Grimblerod, did you hear me?

Trying to contain his rage, Grimblerod grumbles, "How do you know this to be the truth?"

Bardrick discovered the escape last night. We believe he has gotten into Coraira. He had taken the form of a bird, and now we have no idea what sort of disguise he is in. Will you watch for him underground? And let us know of any sightings?

"Why should I help?" the goblin asks. "What do I get in return? Asgall can't harm me anymore."

After what you did with the Caine child, are you really in any position to be bartering with me? Larque raises his voice in anger. *Besides, what is it that you would want? What could you desire more than what we have already given you?*

"What?" Grimblerod grunts. "Do you mean the freedom to pass between realms? That is good, but there is more that I desire... one of the spiders."

There is a pause before Larque speaks. *I'll have to discuss this with Calla.*

"Spider or I will keep any sightings of Asgall to myself."

Larque hesitates. *Fine,* he says. *It's a deal.*

The green stone stops buzzing, and the vision of Larque is gone.

Grimblerod leaves the gems strewn about the lair. This task is far more important. *Nothing is more critical than me getting that spider,* he thinks to himself as he shuffles to one of his openings. *I will find him. And I will have my revenge.*

Grimblerod claws his way up through the damp dirt. His trousers fall to the ground as he emerges, in toad form, above the earth.

How I despise the never-ending sunshine of Coraira, he thinks as he looks for a puddle or cool stretch of mud.

"Plop." A yellow snake falls to the ground from the tree. It slithers through the grass.

An unfortunate toad hops past the snake's wide open jaw. Before the amphibian can escape, a mouth snaps shut around it.

Grimblerod watches in horror. The smell of sulphur fills his nostrils.

Rage rises up inside of him. *Asgall.*

You are out of chances, he thinks as he hops back to his lair, where he will dream about his revenge against the man who took everything from him.

Including his sweet Freya.

CHAPTER THIRTEEN · SLITHER

WITH A stomach full of toad, the snake slides his smooth body up to the trunk of the pixie tree and calls on his desperate servant.

The grimoire is in the sea dragon's cave.

The vision stops her in her tracks as she walks along the bumpy Rhyme terrain. This time, it is not a robin she sees, but a yellow snake. Its body is tightly coiled around a branch.

"I will find it," she says. "Have you made it to Coraira?"

Yessssssss, hisses the snake.

"Wait for me there, at the shore on the eastern edge of the land. I will come to you when I have the book."

But the land is locked.

"I will find a way," she promises.

In the meantime, I'm going to eat as much as I can to gain strength. When you find the book, look for the spell that will change me to my proper form.

"Yes, Asgall, I will waste no time." As the vision of the snake disappears, she adjusts the bag slung across her body. She can now see her destination in the distance.

If she is to gain entry to Coraira, where the sea dragon's cave can be found, she will need some help.

A smile crosses her face as she nears the stone hut with the thatched roof.

CHAPTER FOURTEEN - CONFESSION

DOZENS OF fairies flit around the cheerful Coraira landscape. Some help the honeybees pollenate the flowers. Some bask in the sun. Their translucent wings catch the sunlight, casting rainbows in all directions like hundreds of tiny prisms. Sibley and Cinnamon buzz through the air spreading word of Asgall's escape and requesting that all creatures aid in the search.

"Let's split up. We'll cover more ground that way," suggests Cinnamon.

"Ok," agrees Sibley. "But Cinnamon... don't you feel like at least one of us should be watching over the twins?"

Cinnamon twists his face as he ponders the question. "No, they're safe with Novah for now. We will go to them when we've warned everyone."

FIDGET AND Wink sit on a patch of feathery moss beneath a red-capped toadstool at the entrance to the forest. White and red roses are tangled and twisted around the trees above the mushroom, forming a charming archway to an enchanted wood. Ten fully grown unicorns and six foals graze on grass and wildflowers nearby.

Fidget rests her back against the damp white stem of the mushroom, and Wink sits cross-legged beside her. They are hidden beneath the umbrella-like shade of the fungi.

Fidget tugs a petal from the daisy she holds in her hands. "She'll kill us," she proclaims.

Wink pulls off another petal. "She'll kill us not!"

Pulling off the last petal, Fidget sadly utters, "She'll kill us."

"This is crazy, Fidget. Calla isn't going to hurt us." Wink dramatically swipes at the pile of petals.

Just a short distance away from the pixies, Calla crouches over the stream, filling a small glass bottle with sparkling water.

"There's no point in putting it off any longer, Fidget. Let's go talk to her."

Wink stands and offers Fidget his hand. She ignores the gesture, pulling herself up to standing. The pair bound over to where Calla kneels, screwing the top on her bottle of stream water. The unicorn stands as still as a statue by her side.

The pixies respectfully wait for Calla to address them before speaking to her.

She senses their presence almost immediately.

"Hello Fidget, Wink," Calla says. "Have you brought me Asher's voice?"

"We are sorry, Calla," Wink apologizes. "Grimblerod was in the lair when we were there to find the voice. There were hundreds of crystals, and we didn't know which might be his."

"Did you manage to take one?" Calla asks.

"Yes. Here it is," Wink says.

"Thank you." Calla takes the crystal in her hand. She closes her eyes and tightens her fingers around the green gem. "I do appreciate your help," Calla says when she opens her eyes. "Our magic has limits underground, so your assistance has been essential."

Fidget and Wink smile proudly.

"This voice," Calla says, "belonged to a man who has long been dead. But it will do. We can make adjustments. I need you to bring this to Novah. She will know what to do."

Nodding, Fidget and Wink bounce away from Calla and towards the pixie tree. Wink cradles the green gem in his arms.

"Eew! A snake!" Fidget shrieks, jumping higher than normal to avoid the yellow creature slithering through the grass.

Wink sniffs the air and scrunches his nose. "Fidget, say 'excuse me'!"

"Ok. Why?" Fidget asks. Then she detects what Wink has smelled and crumples her nose. "Wait, that wasn't me! You smelt it, you dealt it!" Fidget's white flower petal skirt bounces up and down as she jumps through the grass.

CHAPTER FIFTEEN · STARLA

LARQUE STANDS at the base of the mountain on the western side of Coraira, where tall peaks stretch up into the clouds.

The damp, pebbly sand crunches beneath the well-worn soles of his black boots. The water casts a blinding light under the full Coraira sun.

The bottom of the mountain is marred with caves of all sizes, carved in the rock by the relentless rhythm of the sea. The water sloshes in and out, making a gulp-like echo in the hollows of the rock.

Before entering the sea dragon's cave, there's someone Larque needs to see. He steps into the tepid water and extends his left hand. A silver orb of light twists around on his palm before turning into a glittering white conch shell. He blows into the conch twice and the sound of chimes fills the salty air.

Larque puts the conch to his ear and listens for a moment for Starla's signal. He nods when he hears it, then shakes the conch with his left hand. The shell turns again into an orb of light, then disappears.

The water around him moves quickly. In the distance, he sees her break through the surface, her skin the colour of chocolate. Then she dives back in, flipping her golden tail up behind her. Within seconds, she has reached him.

"Larque, it has been a long time." Her voice pours from her throat like music.

"Starla, it is good to see you."

Starla sits on the sand, keeping her golden tail in the water. Her thick mane of black hair reaches the sand and spills out around her, strands of blue, silver, and green twisted throughout it. The golden scales of her tail extend all the way up to her breastbone.

"Bardrick says you will hide the pendant," Larque says.

The mermaid clutches something in her hand. "Yes," she says, as she passes the object to Larque. "Put the stone in here."

"Is this what I think it is?" Larque asks, looking down at the object in his hand. It is a purse of black and green seaweed, stitched with gold. It is about the size and shape of a soup bowl, but much flatter. Its clasp is made from a large snail shell.

"Yes," Starla replies. "It is a mermaid's purse."

Larque pulls Elora's pendant from his pocket.

"Is that it?" Starla asks, gesturing towards the pendant Larque holds. "The last known key to Coraira?"

"It is one of them," Larque says. "Freya may still have hers."

"Has anyone any idea of where she is?" Starla flicks her tail in the water.

"No, but the fairies continue to search." Larque places the pendant in the purse. Sewn from enchanted seaweed, a mermaid's purse is a vessel with untold powers.

Larque fastens the clasp on the purse and passes it to Starla.

Starla waves her right hand over the purse. A white light appears from her palm and washes over it.

"Thank you, Starla. And please warn the merpeople of Asgall's escape. He could take any form, and if he knows that mermen and mermaids can travel between realms, he may attempt to embody one of you."

"I will always do what I can to prevent evil from entering Coraira," Starla tells him as she wriggles her golden tail into the water.

As Starla swims off into the deep with Elora's pendant, Larque continues along the shore to the dragon's cave.

When he reaches the mouth of the cave, Larque places his hands upon the cold, wet rock. He creeps inside. He can hear the rumbles of the creature's snores filling the cave. After a moment, he reaches the enormous head of the dragon. Its mouth is as tall as he is. It takes a few minutes for Larque to walk past the dragon's body, to the back of the cave. It smells of damp smoke and salt. He steps past the beast's coiled, serpentine tail, where he sees the glint of the golden chest.

Larque holds his hand over the chest, and the top silently opens.

The soft drip of water echoes through the cave. Larque can hear his breath. The dragon has stopped snoring.

Larque picks up Asgall's grimoire, closes the lid, and turns to face a wall of orange scales.

The dragon's green cat-like eye looks down at him, and its nostrils are flared. Black horns stretch over its orange head. A black and red fin runs down the centre of the dragon's back, from the top of its head to the tip of its 300-foot tail. Each of the dark orange diamond-shaped scales on the back of its torso is about the height of two humans. The front of its body is covered in tall, dark grey plates.

A low growl tumbles out of the dragon's throat. A puff of residual smoke comes out of each of its nostrils.

"Warn the others," Larque says to the dragon. "Asgall has escaped."

The dragon's jaw hinges open, and the creature bares its teeth and uncoils its tail. With a great roar, the beast heaves itself into the water and soon disappears beneath the waves.

CHAPTER SIXTEEN - DESTINY

FIDGET AND Wink perch in a berry bush, near where Novah and the twins are sitting.

"Which one's Novah?" Fidget whispers.

"The one that isn't Ariana or Asher," Wink replies. Wink puts his hands around one of the dark purple berries on the bush and pulls it from its stem. He then uses all of his might to smash it into the side of Fidget's face.

Wink bursts into laughter as Fidget sits, stunned and purple. Using one hand, she wipes her cheek, bringing a scoop of berry flesh to her mouth. She then starts to giggle.

Ariana and Asher both turn to see why the bush has started shaking.

"Fidget, Wink, what are you doing here?" Ariana asks.

"She can still see us!" Fidget whispers loudly, shoving Wink with her elbow.

"What was your first clue?" Wink plucks a petal from Fidget's skirt and uses it to wipe the berry juice off his friend's face.

Fidget bounces over to where Ariana and Asher sit with Novah. Wink follows her.

"What do you have there?" Novah asks.

"Wow, you can see us, too?" Fidget says.

"That's right, dear!" Novah laughs. "I've always been able to see pixies and fairies. But I haven't seen a pixie carrying such an important object before."

"Calla said you would know what to do with this," Wink says, offering the gem to Novah. "It's a dead guy's voice for Asher. Calla says it will do!"

"Well, all right then!" Novah says, clutching the gem tightly in her hand. She turns to Ariana.

"This is the perfect time, Ariana, for you to practice your gift."

"I'm going to give Asher a voice?"

Asher looks unsure, but Ariana is beaming.

"Here." Novah hands the sparkling green gem to Ariana. "Please don't be disappointed if this doesn't work right away. It can take years to master and control your gift."

"What do I do?" Ariana says, taking the gem in her hand.

"Asher, you must wish with all of your might that you can speak," instructs Novah.

I can certainly do that, Ariana hears Asher think. Holding the crystal in one hand, she takes her brother's hand in her other.

"Because we have a voice to give to Asher, this is not the same as simply wishing that he could speak. Do you understand how that is different?"

"I think so," Ariana says. "This way, there is a voice to be transferred to Asher. If I wished for a voice when he had none, it might throw off the balance. So I might lose my own voice, or someone else might lose the ability to speak."

"Such a fast learner! Yes. That's it exactly," Novah says proudly. "Ariana, concentrate on how it would sound to hear your brother speaking to you."

Ariana closes her eyes. Her white streak of hair glows. The pendants both twins wear start to glow, too.

A beam of light shoots from the gem Ariana is holding.

Asher's eyes widen, his eyebrows crawling up his forehead as he wonders what is happening to the gem in his sister's hand.

But Ariana's eyes remain closed as she focuses on her brother's wish. Suddenly, words come from her throat:

"Vox reditum!"

The crystal in Ariana's hand is no longer solid, but has become a million tiny points of light. They float up out of her hand and slowly drift to Asher.

"Open your mouth, Asher," Novah orders.

Asher complies. The beads of light enter his mouth.

Ariana says the words again: "Vox reditum!" This time she opens her eyes. "Asher, you say it, too. Vox reditum!"

His lips form the words and a sound rises out of his throat: "Vox reditum!"

Asher turns to Ariana. "Thank you, Sister," he says, in a a deep voice that doesn't quite fit a thirteen-year-old boy. "I haven't spoken since the day I followed the toad."

"I did it!" Ariana looks in awe at her empty hand.

"Indeed, you did!" Novah says. "Asher, you will have adopted the vocabulary of the person to whom this voice belonged. You may also inherit some other bits of his knowledge."

"How did you know the words to say?" Asher asks with the voice of a grown man. He puts his hands to his throat.

Fidget and Wink erupt in a wild fit of giggles.

Novah glares at the pixies. "That's enough," she says sternly.

"But it's so funny! It's a man's voice coming out of a kid!" Wink rolls around on the ground with laughter. Fidget stands next to him, doubled over and giggling.

"Imagine," Fidget says between spurts of laughter, "if we'd chosen the voice of a girl!" Neither Fidget nor Wink can hardly breathe, they are laughing so hard.

"Shall we make the pixies disappear?" Ariana suggests in a loud voice.

The pixies immediately stop laughing. "Our work here is done!" Fidget cries. She pokes Wink hard in the arm. "You're it!" she cries and bounces off towards the pixie tree. Wink follows behind her.

Asher's cheeks grow red.

"Asher! You can talk! It doesn't matter that you sound like a grown up." Ariana squeezes her silent brother's hand.

"How did I know the words?" she asks Novah.

"Your pendant connects you to your magic," Novah says. "The energy within you is very strong. I knew it would be, but it's much greater than I ever imagined."

"Would it be breaking any rules of magic if I wished Asher to sound more like a boy his own age?"

"No, I don't think that could do any harm," Novah says with a smile. "I'm so pleased that you're catching on so quickly!"

"Asher, hold my hand, and let's both wish that your voice will always match the age you happen to be." Ariana squeezes her brother's hands in hers and closes her eyes, wishing that his voice fit him better.

"All right, but I'm not sure what that should sound like," Asher says in a voice perfectly befitting a young man.

Novah shakes her head in amazement. "It's as if it's completely natural for you!"

None of the three notice that Sibley and Cinnamon have landed in a nearby berry bush, to check on the twins.

"See," Cinnamon whispers, "they're fine!"

"Shh! Look!" squeals Sibley.

"Um, Ariana, what's happening?" Asher asks with his new voice, his gaze fixed on his sister's pendant.

Ariana looks down. The opal in her pendant is glowing. Colours leap out of the stone. Orange and pink and blue threads of colour latch on to one another in front of their eyes. The strands break apart in places and connect in others.

The strands of colour begin to form letters.

"It's a message," Novah says, watching words of a foreign language form before her.

"What does it say?" Ariana begs, trying to make sense of the shapes and letters that sparkle and glisten, suspended in the air. Her hand is still resting on the glowing stone around her neck.

Novah puts up her hand, gently shushing Ariana.

After studying the words for a moment, Novah's expression changes.

The glittering strands of colour dance their way back into the opal.

The smile on Novah's face has vanished. Her skin turns pale. "No," she says. "It can't be!"

"What was that?" Ariana asks, looking down at her pendant. "What did those words say?" Her streak of silver hair glows.

"Do you recall me ever telling you about the land of Coraira, when you were small?" Sibley asks, landing on Ariana's shoulder.

"Sibley!" Ariana smiles. "Um, no. But isn't Coraira where Larque was taking Mother and Father today?"

"Yes." Novah's face softens a little. "Coraira is where the fairies live. It is a world of magic."

"Coraira is ruled by Elora's twin sister, Calla," Cinnamon says, after landing on Asher's knee.

Asher shudders at the mention of the witch's name. Seeing this reaction, Novah assures the twins, "But Calla is as good as Elora was evil." She continues, "Without a ruler in Coraira, magic can't exist. For this reason, there must be a successor, in case something should happen to Calla."

"Novah, what does this have to do with me?" Ariana asks.

Novah takes a deep breath. "Ariana, that pendant of yours will work as a key, to grant you entrance to the magic realm. For it is your destiny to one day become the ruler of Coraira."

"I am to rule the world of magic?" Ariana squeals. "But what about Calla? Isn't she immortal?"

"Yes, she is, but the Ancients are not immune to bad magic or unfortunate mishaps," Novah says.

Ariana notices neither Sibley nor Novah seem to share her excitement.

"What is it, Novah? Why do you sound so disappointed?"

"Because, dear. The keys have a limited number of trips on them."

Sibley speaks again. "Once you go to Coraira to rule, Ariana, you will no longer be able to come back home. You will have to say goodbye to your home and your family... for good."

CHAPTER SEVENTEEN - GRANDMOTHER

"NEVER?" ARIANA tries to make sense of the news. "I'll never be able to come back home?"

"My darlings!" A woman with wild red hair approaches from the front of the hut. She wears a long patchwork skirt and a brown vest over her white blouse. A cloth bag crosses her body.

Having seen that the twins are safely protected by two magic women, Sibley and Cinnamon leave again to continue spreading the news of Asgall's escape throughout the land.

"Grandmother!" Ariana cries, getting up to her feet and quickly racing to embrace Rebecca Caine.

After releasing Ariana from their hug, Rebecca smiles at Asher. "I've come to see my grandson. But this can't be him! This is a grown man, not the four-year-old child I remember!"

Asher looks nervously at the woman, and then at Ariana.

"It's ok, Asher! Don't you remember Grandmother?"

Asher shakes his head.

A flash of pain crosses Rebecca's face, and then she smiles. "Oh, it's all right, dear. After all Asher has been through, he has every right to be untrusting."

Rebecca turns to the woman sitting beside her grandchildren. "Novah, it's been a long time!"

"It has indeed, Rebecca!"

"Novah was teaching us about our gifts, Grandmother," Ariana says. "And about my destiny."

"Then, shouldn't we be happier?" Rebecca asks, noticing the frown on Ariana's face. "Look at those beautiful stones!" She reaches out and touches the opal on Ariana's pendant.

"Coraira opals," Novah says.

Rebecca gasps. "Not like those worn by the Ancients?"

Novah nods. "These children are the next generation of Ancients!"

Rebecca furrows her brow and frowns. "Isn't that quite a lot of responsibility for such young children?"

"Grandmother," Ariana starts, "my destiny is to rule Coraira."

Before Rebecca can say anything in response, the air around them changes. It ripples like water.

"What is happening?" Asher whispers, gripping his sister's hand.

A vision comes into focus.

"Larque?" Novah says. "Is something the matter? I thought you would be here by now. I've already given—"

"Novah," Larque interrupts. "There is news. Asgall has escaped."

"No," Novah says in disbelief.

"When did this happen?" Rebecca gasps. "Do you know where he might be?"

The apparition looks then at Rebecca.

"Larque," Novah says. "This is Rebecca, Lochlan's mother."

Larque nods and continues. "It happened last night when the portal to Darali opened for Elora. Calla and I are making preparations."

"Who is Asgall?" Ariana asks.

"Asgall would make Elora look almost human," Larque explains. "If he is able to regain his full power, we fear he will summon a creature far worse than the Jagwa."

Asher shudders, remembering the shadowy black creatures from the night before. The ones that could stop your heart from beating with just one look at them.

"What can we do?" Novah asks.

"One of you stay with the twins and keep them safe. And hide this." The vision of Larque shoves an object towards Novah. She reaches out and a leather-covered book is placed in her hand.

"Is this—" Novah starts.

"Yes, it is Asgall's grimoire. Calla and I have what we need for the locator spell, but the book is not safe here. Not now, as we suspect Asgall has made it into Coraira."

"Shouldn't it be kept with the other relics?" Novah asks.

"Asgall overheard us talking about the book's location, so I had to retrieve it."

"Why can't you destroy it?" Ariana asks.

"A grimoire such as this one cannot be easily destroyed," explains Larque. "It is protected by magic. Even if it were burned, Asgall would know something had happened to it, and he could make it whole again. It must be hidden, below ground, where our magic is limited. Now, I must go. We have much work to do."

The vision of Larque fades.

Novah studies the grimoire with a look of concern. The image of three dragons is etched into the leather on the ancient book's cover. It is held closed by a brass buckle. "I don't even like this book being in Rhyme. You can smell the evil in it."

"Is that what I smell?" Ariana asks, wrinkling her nose.

"Yes, child. That is the smell of dark magic," Novah says.

"And rotten eggs," Rebecca adds.

"The air here is too rich with magic," Novah says. "I feel it would be safer if this book were hidden elsewhere."

"I could take the grimoire to Valorium," Rebecca offers. "I could bury it underground in a place where it would never be found. I can put a spell on it."

"I should be the one to take it," says Novah. "Larque did entrust the grimoire to me."

"But, Novah, if you leave Rhyme... well... Mother told us that you don't know what might happen since you are so... old. That you're protected partly because of the enchantment of the island," worries Ariana.

Novah sighs and ponders this. "I'm afraid you're right. We don't know what will happen if I leave Rhyme after so many hundreds of years. I'll wait here and explain this to Lochlan and Gwendolyn when they return."

"Can we go with you, Grandmother?" Ariana asks.

"That would be far too dangerous." Rebecca shakes her head.

"Please!" Ariana says. "We've never been anywhere at all! How I would love to cross the sea!"

"Absolutely not!" Rebecca argues. "As much as I would love to take you with me, your parents would never forgive me."

"Yes, they should be returning any time. I thought they would be back by now," Novah says with a hint of concern in her voice.

"Well, we can waste no time, so I must get going with this," Rebecca says, placing the grimoire carefully in her bag. "Why don't the two of you walk me to my boat?"

"Lunch will be ready when you return, children." Novah plants a large kiss on the face of each twin.

"Remember, children, though you are stronger when together," she warns them as they walk to the shore with their grandmother, "you haven't yet gained control of your gifts, so be careful!"

The twins wave goodbye to Novah and continue walking with their grandmother.

CHAPTER EIGHTEEN - THE NOTE

GRIMBLEROD SITS at the small wooden table. The candle drips wax on the parchment, its flame sputtering on the wick.

"Don't go out on me now," the goblin threatens the flame.

He dips his quill again into the bottle of ink. His long fingernails scratch along the parchment as he writes.

The carrier is waiting. He must hurry.

He drops the quill and traces his grubby fingers along the words he has written, leaving behind a black smudge.

Satisfied with his message, he rolls up the parchment and seals it with a bead of hot wax.

He then uses the candle to guide his way to one of the tunnel openings. He waddles quickly, hoping she is still there. Thankfully, she is.

When the small scroll of parchment pokes above the surface, the dove takes it in her talons and flies off to Coraira.

Grimblerod scratches at something behind his ear. After inspecting the crunchy yellow substance, he puts it in his mouth and chews.

Soon I will have almost everything I want. Almost.

CHAPTER NINETEEN - STUNG

GULLS SCREECH across the clear blue sky and over the glittering waves of the sea. The scent of salt hangs in the air, so thick it can almost be tasted.

Rebecca's wild red hair floats behind her on the gentle sea breeze. She continually tucks tendrils behind her ears as they fly across her face. She treads carefully over the uneven terrain, her grandchildren at her side.

"Grandmother," Ariana says as she walks between Asher and Rebecca on their way to the shore, "can I tell you about my gift?"

"Of course, darling!"

"I can make wishes come true!"

"Oh my! Such a powerful and dangerous gift!" Rebecca says. "And what about you, Asher? What is your gift?"

"I haven't tried it yet," he begins, "but Novah says that I can make time stop."

"Asher can also move time move back and forth!" Ariana says.

"Oh dear, that is a dangerous ability to have!" Rebecca says. "If I had such power, I'd be tempted to turn back the hands of time so that I might look like my sixteen-year-old self again—ouch!" Rebecca holds her hand to her neck, her eyes widening in alarm.

"What's wrong, Grandmother?" Ariana cries.

"Bee sting. I'm allergic," Rebecca gasps, putting her hands to her throat. "I did not bring my potion..."

"She can't breathe!" Asher says. "What do we do?"

"Her face is swelling!" Ariana cries, looking at her grandmother's pale features. "Asher, take my hand!"

The twins join hands on the site of the bee sting. A soft blue light radiates from their palms, their pendants, and Ariana's hair. The beams combine and fix themselves on their grandmother's injury.

Rebecca takes a deep breath and exhales, coughing. "You saved me!" she says when she finally catches her breath. "You hold the power to heal!"

"Are you all right, Grandmother?" asks a concerned Ariana. "Should we take you back to the hut so you can rest?"

"Nonsense, I'm just fine. And I'm most thankful for my quick-thinking grandchildren. I never travel without my healing potion—how silly of me to have forgotten it! Let's continue to the shore. I must get this grimoire out of harm's way!" Rebecca pats the book in her cloth bag.

When the trio approaches the pixie tree, Rebecca pauses, out of breath. "Children," she says, "perhaps I do need to rest for a moment."

Asher and Ariana stop walking as Rebecca sits down on the grass. Their pendants lift up off their chests, as if by some magnetic force. The white streak of hair on Ariana's head glows again.

"What's happening, Grandmother?" Ariana asks, looking down at her pendant.

"This, dear, is where the entrance to Coraira is. Now that you both have your keys, you can choose to enter any time you wish—of course, you never know when that one time will be your last."

"We should be getting that grimoire to safety, shouldn't we, Grandmother?" Asher asks.

"Yes, dear. Just one more minute for me to get my wind back—that should be enough rest. You know," Rebecca says through laboured breaths, "when I was your age, I dreamed of seeing the land of magical creatures and unicorns that my mother told me stories about."

"Unicorns?" Ariana can't hide her excitement.

Rebecca smiles as she struggles for another breath. "Mother used to tell me of a magical stream that flows through the land. Of how one drink from that stream could cure any ailment."

"Grandmother, should we take you for a drink from that stream?" Asher suggests. "You don't seem to be doing very well."

"Oh, I don't know. I don't have a pendant, so I couldn't enter," Rebecca protests.

"Ariana and I have a connection strong enough that maybe one pendant will gain us both entry. And you could use the other," Asher suggests.

"We really must get this grimoire to safety. And remember, those stones have a limited number of trips on them," cautions Rebecca.

"Maybe we'll be able to move faster once we get you feeling better." Ariana holds her grandmother's hands.

Rebecca nods, still struggling to get a good breath.

Asher slips his pendant off and hands it to Rebecca. She places it over her head and a smile rises to her lips.

"IS THAT your mother with the children? Where's Novah?" Gwendolyn gestures to the pixie tree as she and Lochlan walk back from the village merchant with a special birthday gift for each of the twins.

"I wonder what they're doing?" Lochlan says.

Rather than walk back to the hut, Lochlan and Gwendolyn head towards Rebecca and the twins.

"REMEMBER, CHILDREN, there's a good chance you won't be able to gain entry without having adequate training," Rebecca cautions.

Asher and Ariana stand hand-in-hand beside their grandmother. The pendant around Ariana's neck rises up off of her chest. "We wish to go into Coraira with our grandmother," she says in a clear voice.

The air around them ripples. Looks of pride cross Asher and Ariana's faces as they walk into the dreamlike scene before them, accompanied by Rebecca.

"DID THEY just disappear into Coraira?" Lochlan gasps, after seeing his mother and children vanish.

"Why would they do that?" Gwendolyn asks. "Lochlan, something doesn't feel right."

"I know," Lochlan says, speeding up his pace and changing direction to head towards their hut. "I have a bad feeling, too. Let's see what Novah knows."

"OH MY!" Rebecca cries. Asher and Ariana remain silent as they take in their surroundings.

A sparkling river reaches to the sea. The lush green terrain stretches all around, interrupted here and there by patches of forest. Rhyme foliage has started changing for autumn, but here everything is green.

Colourful fairies fly about, stopping to study the humans who've entered.

"There are more flowers here than I've seen in my entire life!" Ariana cries.

"What are those white horses with horns?" Asher asks.

"Those are unicorns," Rebecca says. "Now let's head to the stream and get me a sip of water so we can get this grimoire where it needs to go."

The three walk a short distance to the stream. Rebecca kneels on the grass and cups her hands, scooping a mouthful of fresh water into her mouth.

"Are you feeling better, Grandmother?" Ariana asks, trying hard not to be distracted by the flowers and the fairies that flit around in the Coraira sky.

"Yes, dear," Rebecca says, taking a deep breath before standing to her feet. "Let's be getting back. You've been lucky enough to see unicorns and fairies, but the mermaids will have to wait until you're the proper ruler of Coraira!"

"Mermaids? There are really mermaids here?" Ariana asks.

"Yes, but we really should be getting back to the shore with the grimoire."

"Do you suppose just a few minutes more would make a big difference?" Asher pleads.

"You're terribly difficult on an old woman's heart! Let's go. But quickly!" Rebecca says, leading the twins to the eastern shore of Coraira.

CHAPTER TWENTY - DOVE

"SOMETHING IS wrong." Calla stirs the elixir in the small black cauldron. "The potion should be ready by now."

Larque sits at the wooden table in the centre of Calla's sun-filled home as she stands over the stone hearth.

Tucked away in a sunny clearing within the trees of Coraira's enchanted forest, Calla's dwelling is unexpectedly small for the ruler of the land. It is a circular house built of wood and glass. Most of the tall windows that wrap around the home are plain. But the large round windows that adorn the front of the structure, one on either side of the arched doorway, are made of stained glass in patterns of roses and birds.

Vines of bright flowers twist all around the charming cottage. Hummingbirds and butterflies buzz around the windows. Songbirds splash in the stone fountains surrounding the home. Glint munches grass near one of the windows. She's never far from her master.

"Remember, Calla, Asgall is one of the oldest of the Ancients. His magic is great. This is going to take time," Larque says. "If we had his blood, it would be quicker."

Calla looks to her finger, where she poked herself with the needle to get the blood needed for the spell. "Yes, you are right. I'm just growing quite impatient."

Calla twists her fingers through her long silken hair. Her crown of flowers sits on the table next to Larque.

"Has Bardrick messaged back yet?" Larque asks.

"Yes, Panzer did bring a message. Everything at the portal is secure."

Calla nods as a snow white dove flies in through an open window and lands on her shoulder. "Why, hello there," she says, turning to the creature. "What do you have for me?" She pulls a small scroll of parchment from the bird's clawed foot.

She unrolls the paper and her brows furrow as she reads the scrawled message.

"What does it say?" Larque asks.

"It's a message from Grimblerod. It says:

Calla, your father has taken an appropriate form. He is yellow-bellied and slithering through Coraira. In return for this information, I ask for one of the enchanted spiders. Signed, Grimblerod."

"So, we're looking for a snake," Larque says.

"I knew we were, all along."

CHAPTER TWENTY-ONE - REUNION

ASHER, ARIANA, and Rebecca make their way down the grassy path. After a few steps across the smooth black rocks, their feet make a crunching sound on the pebbly sand.

"Where should we look to see a mermaid?" Ariana cries, shielding her eyes from the Coraira sun. "Ugh, Asher! Your foot!"

Asher looks down at his foot and shakes the yellow snake from his ankle.

Rebecca frowns at the creature and stops walking.

Ariana takes a deep breath of air. "Do you smell that? It can't just be the book because it has gotten stronger."

Rebecca reaches into her bag and pulls out the grimoire.

She looks to where Asher has kicked the snake. "I'm afraid that might not be an ordinary garter snake," she says, clinging to the grimoire and holding it closely to her chest.

Rebecca points at the snake. She spits a word at it that the twins don't understand: "Hominis!"

The snake rises from the ground and spins around and around and around, until it is no longer there and a thin, pale man, cloaked in black, stands in its place.

Rebecca smiles proudly as she passes Asgall the book with one hand and shoves the twins at him with the other.

"Grandfather, look what I've brought you!"

CHAPTER TWENTY-TWO - GUT

LOCHLAN AND Gwendolyn burst through the door of the hut as Novah stirs the pot of stew.

"Novah!" pants Lochlan. "The twins. My mother. Disappeared."

"Slow down, Lochlan," Novah says in a calming voice. "What are you talking about?"

Gwendolyn speaks while Lochlan catches his breath. "We just saw Rebecca and the children vanish into Coraira."

A chill runs down Novah's spine.

Novah pulls her shawl down over her shoulders and exits the hut, making her way to the pixie tree with Lochlan and Gwendolyn.

CHAPTER TWENTY-THREE - MAP

"THE POTION is finally ready," Calla says as the elixir bubbles, black smoke rising from the cauldron. "I'll never get used to that smell," she adds scrunching her nose.

Larque sits before a weathered black and white map of Coraira. It covers the top of the table. He runs his fingers over its surface. As he does, the rolling landscape of Coraira turns green. The trees sway in the gentle breeze. Leaves drift up off the paper, gently landing on the table. Larque brushes them away. A thin layer of cloud wafts over the land.

Purple patches of heather spring from the paper. The mountains on the edge of the map turn grey, then climb up from the parchment, hardening and reaching for the clouds. Soft snow forms around the highest peaks.

The line that twists through the centre of the map widens slightly, its clear water sparkling under the sun. Within seconds, the water reaches the edge of the island and empties into the sea. The sharp waves sketched around the island now turn blue and lap against the shore. Salty water splashes off the map onto Larque's hand.

Tiny seagulls soar lazily around the island sky. Their soft cries echo through the cottage.

Calla carefully ladles a spoonful of the locator potion into a round-bottomed glass tincture bottle. She crosses the wooden floor to Larque, walking through a large sunbeam coming in from outside. Dust motes twist and twirl in the air.

"It's ready," Larque says, looking at the living map in front of him.

Glass dropper in hand, Calla releases a single bead of purple potion onto the centre of the map, being careful not to hit a gull.

The purple droplet rolls around on the paper for a moment. It falls into the stream and bounces back out, hitting the pixie tree.

Calla and Larque patiently wait, watching as the droplet slowly moves to the eastern side of the map and lands on the shore with a splash. The bead of potion spreads across the shore. A vision appears in its place. Of a man, a woman, and two children.

"Who could that be?" Larque asks.

"It doesn't matter," states Calla. "Asgall has definitely made it into Coraira."

Calla races out of the hut with Larque, but he stops her. "Calla, it's too dangerous for you to come. What if something were to happen, without a trained successor? I'll go."

"You need my help," Calla argues. "You can't possibly take on Asgall alone."

"But Calla, think about what the consequences might be," Larque reasons.

Calla sighs. "I suppose you're right. Send me a message if you need me." She nods towards the unicorn. "Glint and I will come upon your word."

With that, Larque disappears in a swirl of mist.

CHAPTER TWENTY-FOUR
GRANDFATHER

"WHAT IS happening?" Ariana asks. "Grandmother, who is this and why are you giving him the grimoire?"

Asgall's mouth twists into a snarl. Not quite bald, his smooth pink head is covered with grey whiskers. His clear blue eyes are rimmed red. He wears a black robe that reaches the damp sand. Despite his age, he has few wrinkles.

He rubs his fingers over the brown leather of his grimoire, tracing the outline of the dragons on its cover.

"My precious ones," he hisses. The image etched in the leather begins to move.

"You should be proud of this man, children." Rebecca smiles as Asgall approaches the twins, clutching his book. He prods Asher's arm, sniffs Ariana's head.

"This is Asgall, your great great grandfather," Rebecca explains. "And he is the greatest sorcerer that ever lived."

"But, Grandmother! You can't wish to harm us?" Ariana cries.

"You were never anything more than a step in my plan," Rebecca shouts. "I forced the destiny of your parents. I am the one responsible for them meeting and falling in love. I needed you both to be born because I knew you would have the power to break the curse and bring back my beloved mother."

Her face hardens. "But that all went wrong, didn't it? Thanks to you."

Elora was her mother? Asher's thoughts drift to Ariana. Grey clouds start to move in.

"I'll kill them now," Asgall says. "Their hearts will strengthen me for taking Calla next." He runs a long, sharp fingernail along Asher's jaw.

"I don't think we should do that quite yet," Rebecca interjects. "On our walk to the pixie tree, I injected myself with poison to test a theory. My instinct was correct. Their combined power gives them the ability to heal. Before you kill them, you may wish to extract their powers."

NOVAH, LOCHLAN, and Gwendolyn stand at the portal to Coraira, but none of them can see what's happening in the magic realm.

"Why do you suppose Rebecca and the twins would have entered Coraira?" Gwendolyn asks fretfully.

"I really don't know, dear," Novah says. "Rebecca was taking the twins with her as far as the shore. She was supposed to be travelling back to Valorium with Asgall's grimoire, to reduce the risk of the book making it into Coraira."

"How did you end up with Asgall's grimoire?" Lochlan asks.

"Larque gave it to me to hide." Novah pauses. "I have a feeling that something's not right."

"I WISH that Mother and Father were here!" Ariana whispers softly.

A thick blue smoke swirls around her and Asher as Lochlan and Gwendolyn materialize.

Gwendolyn wraps her arms around the twins.

"Mother," Lochlan says, "what's going on? Why did you take the children here?"

"Well, son. Asgall and I were just discussing how best to extract their powers before we kill them," Rebecca replies, calmly.

"What have you done to my mother?" Lochlan shouts at Asgall.

Rebecca shakes her hands at Lochlan and Gwendolyn, sending them flying backwards. Ariana and Asher rush to their parents.

"Remaneo!" yells Rebecca.

All four members of the Caine family struggle, but their feet are locked in place.

"NO!" Gwendolyn screams, reaching for her children. "Lochlan, free us!"

Asgall walks slowly to Ariana. He lifts her silver section of hair with his fingernail. The girl looks hopelessly at her parents.

"I'm trying!" Lochlan shouts as he flings words into the air. "Amitto! Excido!"

Rebecca cackles, "His magic cannot defeat mine, Gwendolyn dear. You married a weak man. He has no power compared to that which I hold."

"What has possessed you, Mother?" Lochlan cries, struggling to free his feet.

"We loved you, Rebecca," pleads Gwendolyn. "You held the twins when they were days old. You spent so much time with Ariana when she was a little girl, teaching her things and nurturing her. How could you do this?"

Rebecca slowly walks towards the twins. She strokes Ariana's long brown hair and says, "Before any harm comes to you, I had best take your powers."

"Grandmother, why are you being so cruel?" Ariana sobs.

Already wearing Asher's pendant, Rebecca rips Ariana's from the girl's neck.

"Grandfather," she says to Asgall. "Maybe we should kill them now. I'm finding it difficult to concentrate."

"Noooooo," Gwendolyn screams, reaching for her husband.

"Why?" Lochlan demands. "Why are you doing this?"

The twins continue to struggle to free their feet. They try stretching as far as they can to reach each other. But it's no use.

Ariana and Asher look at each other, terrified. *What are we going to do?* Asher's thoughts reach his sister. Ariana closes her eyes and thinks, *I wish we were free!*

Nothing happens.

It isn't working without the pendant, Ariana's thoughts cry to her brother. *Why didn't I think to also wish for Novah? She may have been able to help.*

Or she would be in the same state as we are, Asher thinks.

Rebecca cackles at the sight of the four struggling sets of feet.

"Enough," Asgall states. "It is time."

Rebecca nods. "Just one thing first," she says, squeezing Ariana's pendant. "I wish to be a powerful sorceress, just like my mother."

A thick purple smoke curls up around Rebecca, and the crystal around her neck turns orange like a glowing ember. As the mist moves up over her brown boots and her tattered clothes, she is transformed.

Her patchwork skirt has been replaced by a long gown of purple velvet. Its neckline is encrusted with jewels. The sleeves open widely at the wrists, the fabric draping to the ground. A black cape hangs behind her. Her wild, loose hair is secured now by a thin gold band that wraps around the top of her head.

Rebecca looks down at herself and smiles as she runs her fingers along the fine fabric of her gown.

"We are doing this now," Asgall shouts, placing his fingers on the cover of the grimoire. "Draco spiro!"

The grimoire falls to the ground, and three scaled creatures rise from its cover.

Rebecca brings her hands together as her mouth twists into an evil grin. Asgall simply nods as three dragons rise up and into the air. They stretch higher and higher, casting huge shadows across the shore. The creatures reach seventy, eighty, ninety feet up into the sky.

Blue and white scales cover their bodies. Rubbery black wings rest at their sides. Their white snake-like eyes scour their surroundings. Bumps and horns cover their heads. Steam emerges from their nostrils, suddenly turning the air cold.

Ariana crosses her arms to warm herself. She sees her brother do the same, but then his eyes widen. *Larque!* His thoughts reach hers.

Rebecca and Asgall, so focused on the dragons, do not notice Larque standing behind them.

Ariana thinks, *It will be ok, Asher. Larque will keep us safe.*

Larque extends his hands to the ocean.

The waves begin to swell. The sea turns foamy. Black horns break loudly through the surface of the water, followed by orange scales. The sea dragon's head and torso rise up out of the ocean.

Waves crash violently onto the shore, sending clouds of salt spray up onto the beach and above the cliff. The sea dragon roars at the sight of the blue dragons on the shore as if inviting a battle.

A huge flame shoots out of the sea dragon's throat. It narrowly misses Rebecca but not before singeing the sleeve of her dress.

Asgall and Rebecca turn then and see Larque.

Asgall looks at his dragons and shouts, "Draco congelo!"

All three dragons face the sea and, in unison, they roar, releasing clouds of icy breath from their mouths.

A loud crack echoes throughout the land as the sea surrounding Coraira instantly freezes. Ice creeps up the sea dragon's orange scales until the creature appears to be nothing more than a giant lump of white.

"Solvo!" Larque points to the twins' feet. They feel their feet loosen and run straight to their parents.

Larque frees Lochlan and Gwendolyn next. They run to wrap their arms around the twins. Larque pushes his hands towards the family, putting a wall of rippling air between them and Rebecca.

"Nice try," Rebecca laughs. She snaps her fingers, breaking the protection spell and removing the rippling wall.

"Rebecca Caine," Larque says, keeping one eye on the ice dragons and trying to stall long enough to plan his next move.

"Don't act as if you have not seen me before," Rebecca says.

"But I have not," Larque says. "Except for in the vision earlier today."

"That is where you are wrong. Think way back," Rebecca challenges, but the confused look remains on Larque's face.

"Step aside, Larque, or prepare to die," Asgall sneers. "You have interrupted us for the last time."

"No one is going to die here today," Larque says, trying to reassure the terrified Caine family.

"You may be a powerful wizard, Larque, but you will not defeat us," Rebecca purrs. "Our magic is more powerful than yours. And besides, as a pure heart, you are unable to harm your own daughter."

CHAPTER TWENTY-FIVE - ICE

LARQUE TAKES a step back and looks more closely at Rebecca. "Daughter?"

"Enough with the family drama already! This is taking too long," Asgall shouts. He whistles for the dragons' attention and points at the Caine family. "Glacies!"

The three creatures all make low growls in their throats as clouds of icy smoke roll out of their enormous mouths. Frost crawls along the shore, stretching along the beach and up the rocky cliff. Ice covers the grass. The sparkling stream is frozen solid. The waterfall stops rushing. Every tree branch in the land now wears a sleeve of thick white frost.

Lochlan and Gwendolyn are encased in ice, anguished looks glazed on their faces. Gwendolyn's frozen arm reaches for her husband.

Behind Larque, Asher and Ariana reach for each other in their own ice encasements.

Larque struggles with his footing on the slippery ground.

"You're mistaken," he states. "We never had a daughter named Rebecca."

"Mother came to me in a vision, many, many years ago," Rebecca starts. "She told me everything. Of how you turned me and my siblings over to a goblin to be dispersed throughout the kingdom. I know how you turned her to stone. And how twins were needed to break her from her curse."

Larque's breath hangs in clouds as he listens to her. He sees it then: a small mark on Rebecca's chin, where she'd fallen as a child, deeply cutting herself on one of Elora's broken potion bottles. His magic had helped stop the bleeding, but it didn't prevent the scar.

"Elizabeth," Larque utters in disbelief.

Asgall still stands in front of his ice dragons.

"Enough with the talk." Asgall hurls his words at Rebecca. "Am I going to have to do this myself?"

Rebecca continues with her confrontation, ignoring Asgall. "I have been through several name changes and marriages over the centuries, easily outliving my husbands each time, always with the hope of bringing twins into the world to break the curse. The one time I managed to have twins of my own, one was stolen from me. And that was your fault. It was you who was responsible for my son—Lochlan's brother—being taken from me. YOU!"

How could this witch be my own daughter? Larque ponders, dismayed. "You just admitted you wished to have twins so you could release Elora. Can't you understand why we did not want that to happen? There is a part of this story that your dearly departed mother did not tell you. The reason she wanted to have children was so that she could use you for her spells. I may have saved your lives, doing what I did."

"LIAR," Rebecca screams.

"Sadly, it is true. Elora intended to use you and your siblings for her magic. You never would have survived had I not hidden you! You should be thankful, not vengeful."

Rebecca glares at the twins. "Thankful? I'll show you how thankful I am." She raises her arms at the twins.

"Stop!" cries Calla as she and Glint appear on the shore.

I know it's unsafe for me to be here, but I've waited long enough. You need my help. Calla's thoughts enter Larque's head. *I'll distract them. You get the grimoire.*

In a flash of blue light, Sibley and Cinnamon arrive on the shore. Sibley gasps when she sees the iced Caines. She throws her tiny hands to her face and cries, "What has she done to them?"

"I don't know, but we have to figure out how to help!" Cinnamon whispers.

The ice dragons stare at the unicorn, craning their necks to get a closer look at the animal.

"Calla," Asgall snarls.

Rebecca shouts at Calla, "Hello, Calla. Did you come to be reunited with your estranged father?"

Larque locks his eyes on the grimoire at Asgall's feet. With both Asgall and Rebecca distracted by Calla, he whispers the word, "Venio!" The book slides to him across the icy ground. He quickly picks it up and tucks it in the back of his belt.

Calla climbs down off Glint and stands in front of Asgall.

"You look like your mother," Asgall says. "Are you also as foolish as she was?"

"I'm not interested in chatting. What is it you're trying to do here?" Calla says, calmly.

Asgall takes a number of deep breaths before asking, "Where is your mother?"

"I don't know," Calla states. "She hasn't been seen since you were banished."

"She's missing?" Asgall raises his voice. "But I need her to pay. How can she pay for what she did to me if she isn't here?"

"We'll find her, Asgall, don't worry," Rebecca reassures him. "We have all the time in the world!"

"It is time I reclaimed what was stolen from me," Asgall says in a hauntingly calm tone. He turns back to Calla. "I am sure when we make our move to kill you, your dear mother will come out from her hiding place."

"You cannot kill me," says Calla.

"No we can't," says Rebecca. "But Asgall can displace you."

"I think you would like it in Darali," Asgall scoffs. "Yes, a little sister bonding time would be good."

Do you have it? Calla's thoughts reach Larque.

Yes, he replies with a subtle nod.

Glint gallops to the Caines and lowers her head. Her horn emits a beam of white light at Ariana and Asher, and then at Lochlan and Gwendolyn, cracking the ice all around them. As the four thaw, their teeth chatter against the cold. Sibley and Cinnamon sit on Gwendolyn and Lochlan's unfrozen shoulders.

"Dragons," Asgall hollers, "kill them! Draco, neco!"

Larque tosses the grimoire to Calla. The three dragons leap into the air. One flies towards Larque, the other two, towards the Caine family.

Glint charges at Asgall, but before she reaches him, she points her horn at the dragons and a beam of light shoots out from it, paralyzing the beasts.

As Rebecca watches the unicorn, Sibley and Cinnamon seize the moment. With Rebecca distracted, the fairies hasten over and snatch the pendants from around her neck, then race them back to the twins.

Ariana and Asher place their pendants in their pockets. Sibley sits on Ariana's shoulder, and Cinnamon on Asher's.

The unicorn turns to face Asgall and Rebecca. Her horn once again gives off a bright light. The animal rises up in the air. She throws back her neck, and her body twirls and twists in a white mist.

Lochlan and Gwendolyn hold tightly to the twins. Everyone is transfixed on the sight of the unicorn writhing in the air.

Calla takes a few steps back. Larque joins her and they both hold on to the grimoire. Calla motions for the twins to come closer and the four place their hands on the book.

When the twins look back up at the unicorn, the creature is no longer there. In its place stands a woman.

"Freya," Asgall whispers.

CHAPTER TWENTY-SIX - COVER

FREYA'S SILVERY-white hair is tied in a thick braid that hangs down the middle of her back. She wears a light blue gown embellished with silver. A Coraira opal hangs from a pendant around her neck.

"Mother?" Calla gasps.

"Later, my love," Freya says, placing her hand on Calla's arm.

Rebecca shouts, "I wish Calla to be banished to Darali!"

Freya smiles at her and says, "I am afraid the children have their powers back, Rebecca, and you no longer possess the ability to wish Calla anywhere."

Rebecca charges towards the twins. "I need those pendants back NOW!"

Lochlan stands between his mother and his children. Rebecca sneers at her son.

Ariana nervously faces Rebecca and states, "I wish you were powerless."

"NO!" Rebecca screams, her royal garments returning to the shabby skirt and blouse she wore before.

Asgall lunges for Freya, but the woman disappears from sight, reappearing farther down the beach.

"I wish you to stop!" Ariana cries.

"You cannot escape me!" Asgall moans, his ancient magic overpowering Ariana's. "Dragons, wake!"

The ice dragons shake themselves off and start towards Freya. When the beasts get close, she disappears, reappearing on the shore.

"Everyone, NOW!" Calla yells.

Calla holds the grimoire at arm's length, aiming the cover at the scene before her. Ariana and Asher hold hands, each touching a corner of the grimoire. Larque and Freya both extend their arms in the direction of Asgall and the dragons.

"Us too," Sibley whispers to Gwendolyn.

Lochlan and Gwendolyn, each with a fairy on their hand, touch the grimoire.

In a clear, calm voice, Calla chants, "Malum porter libri!"

The stench of sulphur fills the air.

Asgall glares at Calla. "No!" He throws his hands at her as he is hurled up off the ground. The energy from his palms lands just past Calla, and a small flame begins to burn where it hit the earth.

Larque, Freya, and the twins repeat the words with Calla: "Malum porter libri!" Rebecca, too, is tossed in the air.

Lochlan and Gwendolyn join in: "Malum porter libri!"

Asgall and Rebecca's bodies shrink as they twirl and twist in a beam of light. They spit out vile words, grasping at any last chance to save themselves.

Asgall aims his hands at Ariana and Asher and shouts, "Eo Ire Itum!"

A beam of energy shoots from Asgall and smashes into the twins, knocking them to the ground.

Gwendolyn screams and rushes towards the twins but Calla holds her back, saying, "We need you and Sibley to hold the grimoire, Gwendolyn!"

A bright yellow light radiates from Freya's palms as she focuses her energy on Asgall, shielding him from eliciting any more counter spells.

The ice dragons screech and hiss as they're sucked into the same swirling beam as their masters.

The light carrying the dragons, Asgall, and Rebecca grows brighter. The beings then all turn to light and are shot into the cover of the book. Screams of pain fill the air, and then the land is once again silent.

Larque and Calla look down at the cover of the book.

The image of three dragons is etched in the brown leather of the grimoire. This time, the cover also depicts a nearly bald man in a cloak and a woman with wild hair.

As Freya begins to thaw the frozen Coraira landscape, Calla stares at her and marvels, "Mother, how did I not know it was you?"

Suddenly, Gwendolyn grips Lochlan's arm as she looks around frantically and calls, "Asher? Ariana? Lochlan, where are the children?"

They look to the spot where the twins had been knocked to the ground, but there is no sign of them.

CHAPTER TWENTY-SEVEN - TOMORROW

"ASHER! JUMP!" Ariana screams at her brother.

Something is charging at them. A huge shiny black box on strange wheels with circular beams of light on its face. It makes a roaring noise as it moves towards them at a fast pace.

Asher stands and stares at the object.

"Jump!" Ariana screams again, taking his arm this time.

But before the shiny box on wheels hits them, it veers off to one side while making a very loud honking sound.

There is no more ice beneath them, but there is also no grass. The ground beneath their feet is firm and black. And hot.

It's hard like rock. And smooth, but not as smooth as ice.

It stretches out before them, way off into the distance, like a solid black ribbon, interrupted by yellow stripes down the middle.

"What is this?" Asher asks, tapping his foot on the surface of the black substance.

"I don't know," says Ariana. She looks up then and screams.

Another object comes rushing past in the other direction.

"These things seem angry, whatever they are," Asher shouts. "Let's get out of the way!"

Ariana and Asher run away from the moving boxes until they reach familiar, soft green grass.

"Where are we?" Ariana cries as she struggles to catch her breath. "Where are Mother and Father? What happened to the dragons? To Grandmother?"

"I don't know, Sister," Asher says. "I've been with you the entire time."

The twins look around to get their bearings. A moment ago, they were cowering on the beach in the ice.

They look behind them, searching for a familiar landmark.

"Is that the pixie tree?" Asher asks, pointing to a large tree beside a bench.

"It could be, but it could be any sort of tree," Ariana says. "This can't be the same place we left."

Tall buildings can be seen where the small village once stood. There are towering poles stuck in the earth, everywhere, with thick black strings running between them.

Wooden structures, much larger and more colourful than thatched homes, speckle the landscape.

"Asher," Ariana says, reaching for her brother's hand. "Asher, where are we?"

CHAPTER TWENTY-EIGHT - SPIDER

GRIMBLEROD TRUDGES through the dimly lit tunnel, pushing another wheelbarrow full of dirt into the cave where the boy was kept. Though he has been hauling dirt for hours, he knows he has weeks to go before the hole will be full. He hopes to be able to complete the job himself, without having to enlist the help of the dwarves who never do anything without asking for something in return. He has nothing left to trade.

Grimblerod dumps his load of dirt and turns the wheelbarrow around. The wheel wobbles and squeaks as he pushes it through the tunnel.

His mind starts to drift. He imagines how Asgall will be sent back to Darali. If only he were the one able to do it. To send the monster to Darali. Or even better, what it would be like to—

His thoughts are interrupted by a soft thump.

He drops the wheelbarrow and waddles through the tunnel to one of his chutes to the surface. He grunts as he makes his way to the object. He can see it shining from within its glass bottle.

He wraps his filthy black fingers around the bottle and puts it in front of his eyes.

The spider glitters and sparkles, as if encrusted in diamonds.

Grimblerod picks up the note that landed on the ground with the bottle.

He unrolls the parchment and reads:

Grimblerod,

You have shown us where your loyalties lie.

Think long and hard before you use this object.

What you think you want, and what you really want,

may be two different things.

Calla

Taking the parchment and the bottle with the spider inside, Grimblerod shuffles to the section of the cave where he eats his meals. Once in the corner, he brushes at the dirt, revealing a flat piece of wood. After prying the wood out of place, he reaches into the hole and leaves the glass bottle and the note inside. He replaces the wood and adds more dirt to hide it from sight.

"When the time is right," he tells himself. "When the time is right."

The End

BONUS CHAPTER - TEAGAN OF TOMORROW SNEAK PEEK

"IT'S LIKE she doesn't even see us!" A mischievous grin crosses Fidget's freckled face as she giggles to her companion, Wink.

The woodland pixies tug back and forth on the black edges of an old woman's shadow. Novah, the shadow's owner, kneels over the garden, one hand in the dirt, the other holding a red-handled spade. The sun is setting behind her, and though she is almost perfectly still, her shadow dances a jig under the direction of Fidget and Wink. They grow bolder in their movements as they wait for Novah to look up.

But Novah remains focused on her work. Her grey hair is tied in a messy knot on the back of her head. Her unwrinkled brow is furrowed, and her lips are pressed together. Dirt smudges her cheeks. Every so often, she stops digging, sits back on her heels, and reaches into her pocket for another seed. She rubs the seed between her fingers, smells it, and studies it under the sunlight.

"Whaddaya think she's lookin' for when she does that, Wink?" Fidget ponders out loud. Wink shrugs, and the pixies watch Novah place an ordinary-looking seed two inches above the earth. When she takes her hand away, the seed remains suspended in the air until Novah leans back, closes her eyes, and points her fingers at it. Then the seed turns into a ball of light and shoots into the damp brown earth. A green tendril springs up from the ground behind it.

"I should see if she can do that to you!" Wink teases. Fidget sticks out her tongue in response.

"Sibley and Cinnamon are coming!" Wink whispers loudly. Fidget puts her tongue back in her mouth and whispers, "Hide!" The pixies slide their little bodies beneath Novah's shadow so they can listen to what the fairies have come to say.

Sibley, her blue hair pulled into a ponytail, is hovering in front of Novah's face with her iridescent wings twinkling behind her. "Novah," Sibley asks, "has Larque returned yet with Gwendolyn and Lochlan?"

Novah sets down her garden spade and looks up from her work. "They are all inside. Lochlan and Gwendolyn are in shock. I wasn't able to calm them. Larque is using magic to help them get some rest. What happened? I wasn't able to get any information. Larque gave me these to plant and said he would tell me the story later." She places a hand over her apron pocket.

"What are those, Novah?" Cinnamon asks.

"Perhaps we should tell Novah what happened first; she is clearly quite concerned," Sibley offers.

"It's all right," Novah says. Her kind brown eyes smile, but worry is written over her face. "You should both know about these, anyway. These are seeds from Coraira, and they are only to be planted in the most dire of circumstances, when there is a threat over the magic realm. I know something has happened, but I do not know what it is."

Sibley flies down to study the seed in Novah's hand. "It looks like an ordinary pea seed," she observes. "What will it do?"

"Well, we do not know for certain whether they will do anything. But the hope is that they will yield enchanted plants that will help to keep magic alive, should anything happen to Calla and Coraira." She tosses her head in the direction of the pixies who are now dragging her slight shadow across the grass. "The plants are sprouting as I place the seeds in the earth, so the plan is promising. I have put the soil here under a spell to prevent pixies from toying with the seeds. You know how they love to unplant gardens."

The fairies nod in understanding as they watch the form of Novah swinging from the Caines' clothesline, her shadow hanging by its toes from wooden pegs.

"Would you like a nice cup of tea, Novah? Before we explain everything?" Sibley gently asks.

"No, I need to know," Novah insists, folding her hands in her lap. Cinnamon and Sibley sit on her knees.

Sibley starts to speak. "We don't know what happened between the time Rebecca and the twins left here and the time we entered Coraira with Calla's mother—"

Novah's eyes widen. "Freya?"

"She was hidden in plain sight all along," Sibley says. "As Glint, Calla's unicorn."

"Oh, that clever woman!" Novah remarks. "Things must have been quite serious though, for her to come out of hiding?"

"Yes," Sibley says. "Rebecca deceived everyone. She was actually Elizabeth, the daughter of Elora and Larque. Can you believe that? She and Asgall were working together to control the magic. They wanted Asher and Ariana for their powers. They summoned ice dragons from Asgall's grimoire, and the beasts froze Coraira, including Gwendolyn, Lochlan, and the children. We needed all of the good magic we could get. And I don't wish to think about what may have happened had Freya not assisted."

"No!" Novah exclaims. "Are the twins still frozen? What

can I do? I can't believe I didn't pick up on Rebecca—"

"It's not your fault, Novah," Cinnamon says. "She presented herself as a kind grandmother. And they are not still frozen, no."

Novah places her hand over her heart. "Thank goodness."

Sibley and Cinnamon exchange concerned glances.

"What is it?" Novah asks. "What has happened? What has Larque not told me?"

Sibley tucks a strand of hair behind her ear before speaking. "We all focused our energy on moving Asgall and Rebecca from Coraira. Freya, Calla, Larque, Gwendolyn, Lochlan, Cinnamon, and I succeeded in banishing them. They were sent into the cover of Asgall's grimoire."

"Thank goodness," Novah exhales. "And the twins?"

"Well, that's where this story takes a twist," Cinnamon says as Sibley stares at the ground. "Nobody knows."

Novah pauses before speaking. "What do you mean, nobody knows?"

"They disappeared under Asgall's magic," Sibley explains. "The twins vanished. Into thin air."

"What is being done to find them?"

Sibley explains, "All of the fairies, including us, have been searching the realms since the moment it happened. Freya and Calla are trying to get a location using the Map of Place and Time, but I believe other options are also being explored."

"Speaking of the map, I should go back now to Coraira, to see what we can be doing to help," Cinnamon says, flying up from Novah's knee.

"Good idea," Sibley replies. "I will stay here with Gwendolyn and Lochlan until I am needed."

Novah frowns. "I understand now why I have been asked to plant these."

Sibley looks up, waiting for Novah to continue her thought.

"Asgall, Rebecca, and Elora are gone from the realms. It's the balance of magic. As much as we may not wish it so, light must be countered by dark. Good by evil. A new villain is coming. The Ancients are preparing for the worst."

DISCUSSION QUESTIONS

1. What do you think Asher and Ariana are going to do next?
2. Why do you think Grimblerod wants a magic spider?
3. Do you think we will see Asgall and Rebecca again?
4. What do you think will happen to the grimoire?
5. What surprised you most about *Into Coraira*?
6. Do you think Asher and Ariana will be able to use their powers where they are now?
7. Why do you think Elora turned out the way she did? Do you think it had anything to do with her sister's destiny?
8. How do you think all of the fairies feel about what Calla and Larque did to them?
9. What do you think will happen to Freya/Glint now?
10. Mermaids and goblins can travel between realms. What might happen to them if magic is lost?

ACKNOWLEDGEMENTS

To all of the students I've read to throughout this journey, thank you for your wonderful feedback. And thank you to all of the Prince Edward Island schools, educators, and administrators that have welcomed me. To say this has been an enriching experience for me would be an understatement.

Christine. You have helped me take my stories from "pretty good" to "incredible" (if I do say so myself). Your gift for editing will never cease to amaze me. Thank you for making these books so much better, but thanks more for being my daily sounding board, confidant, and incredible source of love and support.

Sarah. Once again, your artwork has surpassed my expectations. Thank you for helping me bring the story to life.

Talia. Thank you for the tremendous amount of work you're doing to promote the "Legend of Rhyme" series. I'm so happy to have you in my corner.

Chris. The covers are such a huge hit! Thank you for the amazing visuals that are helping the books get noticed on shelves.

Heidi. Again, there aren't enough words to thank you for making my dreams come true. But huge hugs and thanks to you, Adam, and the entire DigiWriting and Blue Moon Publishers crew for taking care of business, so to speak.

Bruce. I'm so excited that the PEI Preserve Company and the Gardens of Hope will be interlinked with this series. I'm proud to call you my friend.

Paul. Thank you for being such a vocal supporter of my work. I truly appreciate all that you've been doing to spread the word about the Legend of Rhyme on an ongoing basis.

Chance. You put my story to music and I can't explain how that makes me feel. I never thought I'd see the day when I would refer to my youngest brother as one of my best friends.

BJ. Thanks for messing with the screens at Indigo and doing everything you can to promote my books. And thank you for breaking your streak of not reading books to make room in your life for the Legend of Rhyme.

Krystal. You're one of my best friends and biggest cheerleaders. Thank you for helping me believe that I had something with that early (horrible) first draft of *Elora of Stone*.

Mom & Dad. Thank you for helping to make these novels possible by being there to take the girls so I can meet deadlines and maintain a few ounces of sanity. Thank you for believing in me and for being such good parents.

Jason. Thank you for your unwavering love and support. And for helping me through all of my writing dilemmas by lending me your "fantasy brain."

Casey. Thank you for helping me find mistakes in my stories and for never getting sick of my books. I still don't know how you can read *Elora of Stone* over and over and over again, but I love that you do.

Shelby. Both you and your sister are responsible for these books ever being written. Your imagination inspires me on a daily basis, and I hope you never lose that spark of creativity!

To all of my family, friends, and neighbours who have purchased books and have come to signings and events, thank you all for helping me to make this dream come to life.

Jaime Lee

ABOUT JAIME LEE MANN

Jaime Lee Mann was born and raised in a sweet little house by the sea in Prince Edward Island. The eldest of four, Jaime Lee and her sister could be found any day of the week playing make-believe on the rocky shore below their home, or in their own personal magic forest. (Their younger brothers weren't allowed to follow them.)

Jaime Lee was drawn to books at a very young age and always had one on the go. She decided as a child that she would write books of her own when she grew up. As she got older, Jaime Lee would bring her notebook and pencil to the beach or the woods and write her stories and poetry there. (To this day, her muse finds her in such places.)

The salty air of her childhood home has provided a wealth of inspiration for Jaime Lee's creative writing throughout her life, and she often finds herself drawn there today. Her second novel was outlined on the same rocks she played on as a child, right below her parents' house.

As Jaime Lee grew older, her desire to write never went away, but it took a back seat as she struggled to choose the right career path. She spent time at university studying English and at college, learning about entrepreneurship. As a new mother, with her husband Jason's support, she decided to stay home to care for their children. This allowed Jaime Lee to start her own business called Mann Made Time, where she worked as a virtual assistant.

Her business did very well and two years after their first baby was born, Jaime Lee and Jason welcomed a second little girl into their family. It was around this time that Jaime Lee transitioned her business to solely provide the type of services she most enjoyed — copywriting and ghostwriting. She called her business Mann Made Copy and was happy to finally have an opportunity to write full-time.

Years later, that business would evolve into a partnership called Manley Mann Media, which Jaime Lee formed with a professional editor by the name of Christine Gordon Manley.

Over the years, Jaime Lee has written about many topics including interior design, ant bait, meal-planning, gluten, computer software, and Disney World. She has also ghostwritten manuscripts for all types of people with many different stories, and some of those manuscripts have gone on to become published works.

In 2014, Jaime Lee decided to dust off her dream of publishing her own works. She submitted her children's picture book, *A Bug Is A Bug*, for publication with Toronto publishing company Blue Moon Publishers. The manuscript was well received, and that title is expected to be published in 2016. In the meantime, Blue Moon Publishers has also opted to publish a series of middle grade fiction novels Jaime Lee dreamed up while telling bedtime stories to her daughters. The first book in the "Legend of Rhyme" series, *Elora of Stone*, was the first novel to be published with Jaime Lee's own name on the cover.

When Jaime Lee isn't writing (for herself or someone else), she can most likely be found playing Barbie with her daughters, working out at the local kettlebell studio, or in the kitchen making something delicious.

Jaime Lee is currently working on the third instalment in the "Legend of Rhyme" series. You can read more on her site:

Jaimeleemann.com

or connect with her on:

Twitter: twitter.com/jaimeleemann
Facebook: facebook.com/JaimeMann
Pinterest: pinterest.com/jaimeleemann/
Goodreads:goodreads.com/user/show/34635028-jaime-lee-mann
Instagram: instagram.com/jaimeleemann

Jaime Lee greatly appreciates you taking the time to read this work. Please consider leaving a review wherever you bought the book, or telling your friends or blog readers about the "Legend of Rhyme" series, to help spread the word. Thank you for your support.

WRITE FOR US

We love discovering new voices and welcome submissions. Please read our submission guidelines carefully before preparing your work for submission to us. Our publishing house does accept unsolicited manuscripts but we want to receive a proposal first and if interested we will solicit the manuscript.

We are looking for solid writing - present an idea with originality and we will be very interested in reading your work.

As you can appreciate, we give each proposal careful consideration so it can take up to six weeks for us to respond, depending on the amount of proposals we have received. If it takes longer to hear back, your proposal could still be under consideration and may simply have been given to a second editor for their opinion. We can't publish all books sent to us but each book is given consideration based on its individual merits along with a set of criteria we use when considering proposals for publication.

THANK YOU FOR READING
INTO CORAIRA